The First
Wolf Pack

A Dog's Fable

J. Daniel Reed

First edition November 2021

ISBN 979-8-9850592-0-5 (paperback)
ISBN 979-8-9850592-1-2 (e-book)

Published by Terra3 Communications, LLC
www.terra3communications.com

*To my wife, Barbara, who encouraged me to write
this story with loving support and persistence
that never tired, including her many careful reviews
and edits to this work. She also worked tirelessly
to accomplish all the tasks necessary
for self-publishing—amazing.*

*This book is also dedicated to my parents, Walter
and Margaret, who were inspirational examples
of what it means to love genuinely, live honestly, think
deeply, work diligently, and persevere endlessly.*

Preface

While driving back from Northwestern Memorial Hospital in Chicago in the summer of 2010 my wife, Barbara, asked me to tell her a story to take our minds off our struggles. My mother, Margaret, was undergoing an experimental heart valve procedure that might save her life. Everyone who has had the honor to care for an aging and ill parent knows how stressful it can be but we persevered out of love, respect, and responsibility. The surgery would be successful.

The story I told Barbara that day was about two ancient wolves of incredible power and intelligence who formed the first-ever wolf pack. Barbara loved the mental and emotional picture I painted so she encouraged me to write down my creative musings. From time to time for years afterward we spoke about the idea of turning the story into a novel, but it remained only talk until the day Barbara presented me with a special birthday present—a framed lithograph of a wolf howling into the night sky with the frost of its breath collecting before it. She named the wolf in the lithograph and had me hang the artwork in a place where I would see it often. Barbara said she wished it to be an inspirational reminder of my story about those two ancient wolves so that someday I would write the entire, much larger story that she knew was lurking inside of me.

As life sometimes provides each of us with a strong current, too powerful to resist, my time and energy were consumed with my career as a corporate real estate professional. But the story would not be forgotten. Not too long after receiving my special birthday gift, I began to spend a small amount of time on weekend mornings typing out ideas until the story took significant shape, expanding in its own importance such that it demanded to be told. Having spent decades working on complicated real estate documents of many varieties, and working with many brilliant attorneys, I loved the mastery of language in the written form. While working with construction plans and financial analysis made commercial real estate varied and satisfying, it was the language skills part of commercial real estate I liked best.

Recently my job was eliminated as result of a corporate acquisition so the time had come to apply myself to authorship as a new job. I quickly discovered a labor of love and a big story told itself through my ten fingers.

This novel is the history of the first wolf pack as told by a modern dog named Bingley. Our narrator, temporarily granted the ability to "speak human," tells the dog and wolf version of our shared history you only partially know. It is their story of how the most important foundational truths shared by both *Canis lupus* and *Homo sapiens* were established and spread. This novel, filled with symbolism and action, is much more than just a story of two ancient wolves and the members of their first pack—it's about overcoming our shortcomings to discover timeless and immutable virtues.

The story's narrator was named after the first Airedale Terrier we adopted decades ago who had the heart of lion and the gentleness of a lamb. You just wanted to be sure you met him on one of his lamb-like days. A magnificent creature, he bonded with us in a deeply profound way helping us to imagine if any animal would have an immortal soul, it would be the dog.

The First Wolf Pack was written to entertain animal and historical fiction lovers with anthropomorphized characters who will hopefully remind you of people you know and perhaps, too, you will find a bit of yourself in some of them. As the heroes try to help their species overcome a miserable existence, they discover The Wolf Ways, a set of wolf-virtues and skills that speaks volumes to us today.

After reading this book, you may well think it is possible this story is more history than fiction. You may further wonder if it more accurately tells us what actually occurred thousands of years ago, rather than what we currently believe from certain of our foundational myths.

It has been said many times that in the final analysis each of us in the human family, inside our hearts and souls, are very much alike. This story will also challenge you to wonder if wolves and humans may be very much alike as well.

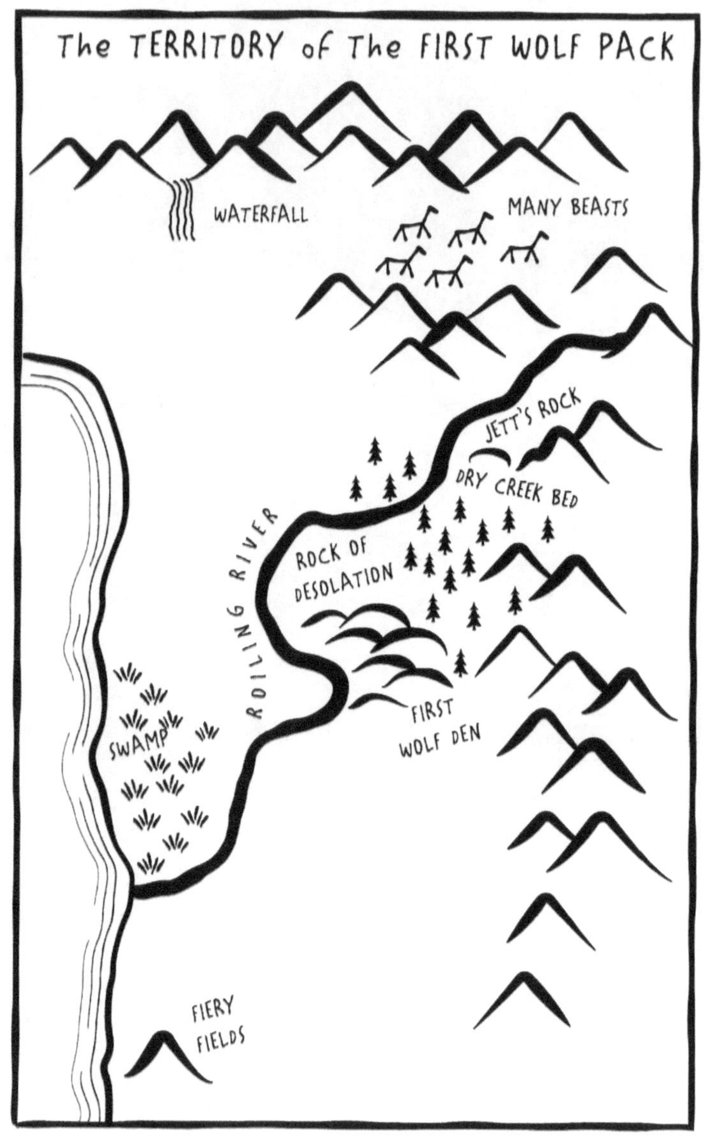

The TERRITORY of The FIRST WOLF PACK
WATERFALL
MANY BEASTS
JETT'S ROCK
DRY CREEK BED
ROILING RIVER
ROCK OF DESOLATION
FIRST WOLF DEN
SWAMP
FIERY FIELDS

The Wolf Ways

Cooperation ("if one is to live,
we both must live" to enable trust)

Trust (to enable loyalty)

Loyalty (to enable tolerance)

Tolerance (to enable self-control)

Self-Control (to allow discernment)

Discernment (to enable gratitude)

Gratitude (the foundation of
unbreakable loyalty to the pack)

Honesty (for the survival of The Wolf Ways)

Alpha Leadership (to ensure the
survival of the wolf pack structure)

Persistence (to test the alpha and keep leadership strong)

The Wolf Den (to ensure the survival
of each individual pack)

The Inhibited Bite (to remember the fight
against the poisoned blood)

1

From the Old Land, a place of rain, rocks, peat, and poets my family comes. Born of a long line of English terrier dogs with blood lines evolved over many centuries and beyond, I am called Bingley. With manipulated genetics, I maintain a pure and sincere wolf core, like all modern dogs—be they herding, fielding, or working specialists; or even if they be couch potato companions. For you see, we are wolves, too. We dogs (*Canis familiaris*) and the wolves (*Canis lupus*) have virtually identical genetics, enough so that we may successfully mate. We share ancient ancestors. The blood of the wolf still runs through my veins.

For countless millennia, irrevocably committed to honor our inheritance, all wolves have remembered The First Wolf Pack. We have passed down to every canine generation The Wolf Ways they developed. These lessons, built on the greatness of our ancestors, have served us well. The Great Wolf

Spirit has declared that it is now time for you to know this history. Thus, I have been given the ability to speak to you in a way you will understand—an ability given to last only long enough that I may share with you wolf history.

While innumerable generations of our ancestors have lived together, never before has my race offered you humans a glimpse into the founding and the profound impact of The First Wolf Pack on both of our species.

All the wolves, the wild and the new, know that the story of our domestication told by your race is not exactly right. Maybe it would be more accurate to speak of how the ancient wolves joined your ancestors; perhaps I should even say helped enlighten them.

It is good for you to know we actually came together because of the decisions made by cunning, ancient wolves. It is for your benefit as individuals and the benefit of the entire human race that I share with you the legend of The First Wolf Pack, a momentous and fortuitous gathering of very superior creatures, each of whom you will meet. In this legend many heroes deserve recognition not for their acclaim, but for your edification and the promulgation of truth, a very special group of wolf ancestors who changed the world.

Uniquely distinct from all other animals except for you, we the new-wolves found our lives intertwined with yours, cooperating with humans from the start of your civilization. Many of your race believe that you domesticated the wolf and created—by your intellect and experimentation—the modern dog, which is so, but you must understand there are no common dogs. We, like you, are all unique individuals with strengths and weaknesses, personalities and styles, which makes every one of us special—just like you. We are products of our breed, our bloodlines. Designed for purpose, we are also products of our environment and training, but most of all we are of that gloriously special thing that has its essence in the wolf spirit we share.

As for me, your humble canine servant, my nearest ancestors came from the region of the River Aire, Yorkshire, with my very existence based on purpose. From vanquishing rats to river otters, I have the heart of a killer, yet a heart with instincts now tempered toward human advantage, fostering our eventual partnership. Now living a comfortable modern life, I retain my stout heart, canniness and intelligence. I can herd your flocks, protect your farm or home, retrieve your game, and track boars. I can join the hound pack to give it some fight, and I can even fearlessly track cougars and bears.

Within your apartment or on your farm I can guard your babies and youngsters with sweet gentleness, giving my life in their service if needed. With a dense two-part coat, I can withstand cold and storms yet offer a perfect surface for a quick nuzzle from my two-legged pack members. Give me a job to do without cruelty, train me with a leader's fair and firm hand, and I will give myself wholly to you. I will be at your side seeking your leadership and approval for as long as my heart beats. From my very core I seek to be of one heart and soul with you, loyal forever if you earn it. But it is also true that while I will not lie, I can quickly learn how to dominate and manipulate the ignorant, the untruthful, or the insecure.

Rising from long and varied lines of terriers specialized by your ancestors, my more distant ancestors were working dogs with ancient blood from great mastiff dogs and fabulous sighthounds. But all of us—my modern terrier and non-terrier cousins alike, along with the ancient dogs you do not know—originated from a place and time of legends, a place where the great wolves roamed the earth in magnificently-efficient packs with whom no other beasts could compete, including your ancestors. For until then no other earthly creatures had learned how to live together, hunt together, and protect one another like the mighty wolf pack founded by The Magnificent Ones. The First Wolf Pack presents the foundational account of today's wolf and reveals the origins of we new-wolves, the dogs you know and love.

Come back with me to days so ancient that only the wolf can remember events as they really happened. For we have not human-type pride to color our memory. We are creatures of pure mind and spirit. We do not know how to spin long and fanciful yarns; we do not stoke our egos with fanciful tales born of self-serving puffery. We only know what is now and what was. With unblemished sincerity we live in each moment guided by the foundation of our eternal wolfenness.

Solitary beings, the earliest of my ancestors were lone wolves. They trusted none, suspected all, and had no interaction with other wolves except for horrific, sometimes mortal, battles over prey or territory. Except for conjugal moments when the season was upon the bitch, each lived alone. But even mating could in an instant turn to vicious battle with severe injury or death.

While we have abandoned the ways of the lone wolf through the discoveries of our first wolf-heroes, it sometimes haunts us when the ugliest of primal blood is awakened. The new wolf and the old, each use The Wolf Ways to control that poisoned blood. These are the wise and noble ways that tie us together.

So, my friends, I will now tell you how our ways originated. With this story comes a warning for the gentle of spirit; nature designed powerful carnivores for a violent life. We survive at the expense of many other lives. Our history does not whisper pleasantly in delicate ears, nevertheless, it rings true to our nature, a predatory drive tempered only by The Wolf Ways.

2

Within a mist-filled valley between hills of sweet grasses and thicket, dotted with oak trees and cool evergreens, epic history was made. Early in the seventh age of our beloved earth solitary wolves roamed the forests and fields, mountains and valleys, streamsides, and shorelines surviving by immense strength and unforgiving suspicion—but always alone.

They lived short and bitter lives, battling mighty foes and each other in the eternal struggle to survive. Their lives were only brief glimpses in time, a few seasons until death, with no beast or human to mourn a single wolf's soul. Back then, my race enjoyed neither joy nor optimism. And these hate-filled competitors found the greatest mortality at the jaws of their own species. This was to change for had it not been so, none of us would be here to enjoy the fruits of this wolf history.

In a perfectly temperate place there lived Versa, the mother of wolf progress. A she-wolf of tremendous cleverness and seemingly unlimited strength, she could run down any deer, fight off any bear, and survive any winter storm, for she was the first great one. Her ebony coat of rich fur subtly shined in the day and glowed like the blood moon when the sun slept. Her perfect black nose was complemented by steely silver-blue eyes, not yellow as other wolves, welling up with intelligence and wisdom that pierced all that fell within her gaze. With a long straight back, stiff as the strongest steel, waving at its end a tail of lustrous fur streaked with bits of gray, Versa stood alone. All other wolves could detect her wolf perfection by the emblems of her body within the air as it carried her scent. No other wolf would dare intrude on her territory except for the bravest male when the pheromones of reproduction drove them mad enough to venture near her.

In the same land separated by a cluster of hills and in the same moment of antiquity lived Arn, a young male wolf standing forty-eight inches at the withers. His coat of silver-gray fur gracefully covered a powerful bundle of muscle and sinew that even the great Versa must have feared. For no wolf had ever possessed the strength, courage, and intelligence of Arn. With a well-sprung chest cavity containing massive, efficient lungs and heart, the greatest of all wolves could run faster, jump higher, and bite harder than all before him. Large paws that could fill a bear's tracks were tipped with hard, black nails that prevented Arn from losing his footing. With ghostly yellow eyes he could focus to the horizon's end in the faintest starlight; all wolves now carry the color of his eyes. Only could one so magnificent and so strong emerge as the father of the greatest of survival squads.

Somehow fate had brought these two superb, but independent animals to a unique place of valley, hills, and streaming waters at a fortuitous moment in time to change a race forever and influence all creatures living in their domain.

Eventually Versa and Arn would not only bring many wolf pups into the world, they did something no wolf had done before—lived together in harmony. But it would not begin well, so first I must tell you how it started. One is always well-served to start at the beginning, at least that is how we wolves know it to be best. By doing so our story has never changed, never wavered from adroit accuracy.

These two powerful wolves competed with one another for the game they tormented and ravenously consumed. All other wild beings within their portion of Mother Earth trembled in fear of the wolf, but especially in the contiguous domains of Arn and Versa. Their world held animals of cloven hoof, ground mammals, and small carnivores that only existed at the pleasure of Arn and Versa. But these powerful sovereigns of their personal domains could not tolerate another wolf competing upon the borders of their worlds. Thus, they stalked one another prowling, contemplating, and scheming how to eliminate the hated rival. But meanwhile each, within the depths of their instinct to survive, also feared the other so evenly matched in stature, power, and ferocity were they. Canine perfection existed in these two.

The dew gleaming upon the grass and leafy canopy presented a morning of crisp cool air, the kind that fills lungs with enthusiasm, making all creatures take deep inhalations. This sunlit morning caused birds to sing just a bit louder and filled flying hearts with wonder. So, it happened on this cold and wet morning when all creatures huddled together for warmth and fear of the wolf, something fateful and momentous occurred.

Daybreak found the great Arn chasing a bull stag carrying twelve points of now-shedded velvet root, about to drive it over the crest of a hill. At the same time, on the opposite, long-shadowed side of the same hill Versa accelerated. She, in full sprint right on the tail of an ibex, used her speed and strength to her advantage. Versa knew the labor of the long, steep climb soon would prove exhausting for her prey.

As the two independent chases converged then collided, one fearful creature changed direction toward the woods, the other to the open field. Arn and Versa reacting to the moment went toward the field, after the struggling ibex. Each dealt their deadly blows on the doomed creature simultaneously, one on the left and one on the right, ending the hunt and kill with speed and precision neither had experienced before. Physical strength laid upon a foundation of a killing lust proved formidable in solitary performance, but in tandem, completion of the carnivores' survival act became profoundly effortless.

They growled and snarled at each other as they butchered their individual share of this feast, using powerful canines to separate their portions, dragging off the shared wolf-banquet to eat alone. Great premolars crushed bone with ease as they feasted on marrow the way you humans feast upon nuts at the end of your evening meal. Resting in near solitude, neither losing sight of the other out of some competitive suspicion or some instinctive curiosity, their great intelligence began to conjure up new, uncomfortable ideas. For the first time in the history of earthly existence did two wolves hunt together. And for the first time the lone wolf was not so blinded with rage at the near proximity of a competitor that it did not seek to immediately annihilate the other. Was it respect, fear, or uncertainty that found its way into the hearts of two lone wolves in the time of ancient hatred? The answer is unknown to us. But our race has never forgotten its importance, for it was only because of this instantaneous truce that our story may be told.

Thus, Arn and Versa began to keep proximity with each other, first at a great distance but always within range of their senses. Slowly and cautiously with great suspicion their domains began to overlap. Distances heretofore much too close for lone wolves to tolerate soon grew commonplace for them as they continued to cogitate on the event of an instant and effortless meal. Why would the two most feared and powerful of all the lone wolves that ever roamed the earth now tolerate each other? Our legend does not explain this, but we and you still celebrate it in the way of our lives.

As their close proximity became tolerable, unsuspecting creatures came between the two wolves. The accidental collision of two separate hunts as an event of randomness was suddenly replaced by an intentional hunt together. When the unsuspecting prey entered a small valley between where they both lay, Arn and Versa caught a glimpse of each other's keen focus as their eyes met. Simultaneously they rose. Movement so quick with non-retractable claws gripping earth and vegetation under the powerful torque as if part of some greater mechanism they lunged. A wolf-work ballet occurred without rehearsal or choreography, but nevertheless as coordinated as those of your practiced professionals on their way to championship glory. Against two wolf bodies nearest to perfection ever known, the creature could not escape.

Some hunts were easy and they were well-fed with time to rest, alone but near enough to keep a watchful eye on the other. Levels of success unknown to the lone wolf became expected. No longer were the exposed ribs shadowing through great fur. The squalid reminder of solitude was forgotten as muscle grew and health expanded.

But not all the hunts were successful. It seems when one wolf ran left, the other ran right and their quarry would escape by running to safety right between them. Or sometimes Arn pushed his prey to the river where he thought he could gain the advantage, but before reaching the water, Versa came over the hill running streamside on an angle allowing the frightened animal to dart away from the river and into the woods where it escaped. While hunting together required a set of skills unknown to them, somehow they found a way to take larger game more often, but not often enough to fully quench the ancient hatred of the lone wolf.

After three failed hunts in a row, Arn's eyes almost glowed with hate as he watched Versa at a distance. Dissatisfaction and bitterness grew as his stomach began to ache with hunger. He thought of the great amount of energy expended without nourishment. In his mind, Arn began to replay again and again memories of recent failures. In each instance he only saw how his brilliant efforts were destroyed by hunting's adversarial partner. So, too, it was with Versa. She was absolutely certain her ways were superior and success was repeatedly ruined by Arn.

In the midst of their newfound prosperity, they now viewed success as an entitlement. Thus, the bitterness and anger of lone wolf blood began to build in each of them until only animosity existed.

A fight was inevitable, a fight of intolerance to determine the most cunning and ultimate hunter. Now we are not proud of this moment in the evolution of our species, but we have never forgotten it, nor the painful sum of its parts.

The poisoned blood of the lone wolf could only be suppressed for a time, even in the face of bounty. Thus occurred a fight of such ferocity that the fields and woodlands shook with the power of the battle, and with it so did all of the other creatures living there.

The fight of The Magnificent Ones went on day and night, each refusing to give up. Certain of their righteousness, their greatness, and driven by the poisoned blood of the lone wolf they fought. Powerful jaws drove fangs into the thick and tough skin covering each other's muscular necks. Teeth clenched upon forelegs attempting to crush the leg bones of the other while blood gushed unceasingly from torn flesh. Spinning moves to reach and rip open exposed abdomens were tried repeatedly. Every muscle straining to gain advantage they battled with nearly limitless strength.

So horrible but evenly matched was the battle, after two days and nights they collapsed exhausted, almost drained of life. If not for the strength of these nearly-perfect creatures gained by their successes together, both would have died as they laid there.

In the throes of death, Versa felt regret for the fight and for her narcissism that allowed her to find fault only with the other. She pondered how the utterly useless hate consuming her would now result in her demise. But as the two wolves each lapsed in and out of consciousness, something started to happen that would change everything. Just as they previously rose in unison to hunt, they now began to lick each other's wounds.

By either instinct or divine guidance each summoned the strength to help the other, to soothe the wounds and slow the bleeding. So, as they rested and tried to help each other heal, some strength returned to them. Bruised and battered, in unison they dragged their injured bodies to the nearby stream that first gave birth to the battle, but now might give them lifesaving water to drink. Each lying there, nearly dead from their wounds and the exhaustion of battle, the water would help. Sharing a silent fear, each considered whether this life source would be enough to save them. The Magnificent Ones' courage and determination stood perched on the edge of abandonment, each now certain they would perish.

Just then, a shimmering fat-bellied trout swimming against the current of the stream jumped a small waterfall, but its pitch was thrown off by the powerful current. Or perhaps it was a great gust of wind that changed its course as the submariner broke the surface tension of its liquid environment. It landed against a bare rock and bounced left onto the streamside earth where it might have flipped and flopped until wet again. But it landed where Arn lay, right between his tattered forepaws. Seeing this, but consumed with futility, he was certain he would die. Or perhaps with charity produced by glimpsing into the face of approaching death he mustered the last of his strength to push, with his scarred and torn muzzle, the errant fish to Versa. She, too, near death, pushed it back to Arn. Reacting to this incongruous gift from Versa, his likely executioner, his life's spirit revived. This she-wolf who would cost him his life, but then licked his wounds, now made an effort to save him. He began to eat. After a bit, he pushed half of the savior-fish to Versa, who also ate. And they lived.

In the throes of death, The Magnificent Ones saw something they had glimpsed in the sharing of a fish and moments earlier when they licked each other's wounds. They saw what it meant to provide food to their partner; it meant life. And so began the pack, to provide care, food, and life to their partners and offspring. Certainly, neither could survive alone in their tattered state. But the will to live, the most basic quality, the natural and inexhaustible commitment to preserve life reared its head within each and would not be denied. A great life bond was formed in impossible irony, a bond that sprung up within two malicious wolves on the cusp of death. So it was in the failures of hatred the great wolf pack began.

Now I can stop here as you glimpse into only a part of this story, but this was just the beginning. Perhaps it is also my inevitable English verbosity or perhaps the result of being the first wolf to be granted the right to speak to you in your language, but more likely it is both of these and more that make me unwilling to stop my storytelling. So driven, I shall eagerly persevere in sharing with you the story of The First Wolf Pack.

Soon, incredibly successful survival concepts paradoxically founded upon the near-fatal fallacy of hate would be discovered by Arn and Versa and then give rise to The Wolf Ways. We the wolf and you the humans share these lessons of immeasurable value. Along the way there is much for you to learn about us. Wolves are not just any race, they are a race of creatures that work together, play together, and stay together like none before. This would make the perfect team, the perfect survival unit, the wolf pack.

3

How was it that two wild and brutal carnivores fighting for two days and nights did not kill each other? Our legend hides this primeval secret. Perhaps it was the strength gained by their joint hunts or perhaps something more magical. Perchance it was the superior life-spirits of Arn and Versa that somehow were greater than all other canines that kept them alive. This superior spirit can be for minor things or the profound, only we wolves know them all.

As they rested, they found warmth in each other's bodies to survive the coldest nights. Almost crippled by battle they ate worms, insects, and berries. They caught small prey by quietly lying in opposing hiding places, one using the flash of a battered paw to scare a rabbit into the jaws of the other. Like the event of the first fish, they shared food and life. Now Versa remembered observing the lynx using stealthy stillness with great success on smaller prey. She began to think higher thoughts, the solving of problems through observation, recollection, and application to current circumstances. Her intelligence served as the foundation for all that followed—a gift from our great canine mother.

Some of our species use the gift of incredible vision to see only the slightest movement at great distances and to see this in even the faintest moonlight. Others have the keenest olfactory sense, able to detect the tracks of animals hours, days, or even months old through storms and wind and snow. And yet others hear so well they know the sound of a falling tree or successful hunt many miles away. But only Arn and Versa had all these gifts, powerful and immense bodies, plus minds so clever they could put them all to use at once in the most efficient combination since terra firma first saw life upon it. And Versa led the way by her insight into stealth that helped them survive during their now accelerating recovery.

As their bodies healed, the great pair began to hunt larger prey again. They now planned, they strategized, and then they executed with deadly precision. By watching great raptors, Arn acquired the understanding of vectors. The combination of speed and direction when properly understood would result in shorter hunts, better results, and less danger to themselves. Versa with her magnificent snout showed Arn how to turn wind direction into an ally, carrying the scent of unsuspecting herds of herbivores toward them and making the great wandering beasts unable to detect the wolf pack until death fell upon their quarry. Arn and Versa realized that using these two understandings were directly related and thus immensely effective. But most importantly, they were using higher thought processes to plan and implement their combined knowledge in a coordinated way in pursuit of a common goal.

Wolves are crepuscular creatures, hunting best just before the break of day and again upon the end of day when light weakens so only the keen eyes of the wolf can see well enough to hunt. Supported by their sensitive ears, wolves know much more about their environment than you might imagine. Their extraordinary vision and hearing were surpassed by an ability to smell everything that ran, crept or flew upon, beneath or above their land. For us it is like the perfect truth of a gust of wind carrying on it the smell of prey, death, or danger. We do not know from where it comes, but it is nonetheless real to us. Have you not seen one of us enthusiastically raise our nose to the air in wide-eyed curiosity while you detect nothing? Together these three wolves' senses combined to unleash a savagery of heart that when focused would not permit safety to any animal in the wolf's domain.

Now these two ferocious lone wolves were onto something special together—teamwork. How else would you explain how a sheepdog willingly and successfully helps the shepherd or a bird dog flushes and retrieves fresh bird meat without first devouring the tasty mouthful? Partners, each playing their role in support of the other by solving problems, would become a timeless truth of the wolf pack. Cooperation was the first Wolf Way. But the old ways of the wretched blood would not yet be denied even with their new successes. The insatiable instinct to be dominant wrestled with their new-found way, for the arrogance of the lone wolf gave no consideration to the significance or life of others.

My dear human friends please stop here and realize the blood of that first wolf pack courses through my veins too. The ways of the wolf, both the despicable and admirable, form the very fabric of who I am. Few of us function well alone; we function and are fulfilled in cooperation with others, especially when we follow a true leader. But many of us could survive alone should enough of the ancient blood of the wolf be found within us and circumstances demand.

For Arn and Versa, there was still a problem festering somewhere in their selfish individualities of countless generations of loneliness; there was the issue of why any wolf would let another lead. While they became more efficient hunters, not every attempt was successful, not every vector understood, not every breeze accounted for. Risk was always present when it came down to the kill, particularly the taking down of creatures larger than themselves with great horns of piercing ivory able to eviscerate a wolf's belly.

On one such hunt, a great buck was selected and pursued, for a brutal winter was nearly upon them, and they desired copious meat. The sound of the rut resounded throughout the land as deer honed their antler points on trees until these vestiges grew as lethal as your ancestor's spear points. Arn and Versa, using their powerful and now healthy bodies, quickly ran down the great buck with the tactics they discovered, but something went wrong. They both went for the same hindquarter, and knocking the great buck to the ground, they, too, stumbled. Quick on his feet this great deer turned his rack of ivory and drove it right toward Versa's exposed abdomen. Somehow, Arn wedged himself between them and he instead was gored upon and below his rib cage, fortunately by only one of the many antler points. Two inches more to his exposed belly and Arn would be mortally wounded, to die a slow and painful death. Versa leaped upon the great beast's back, taking the top of its neck into her powerful jaws, knocking the stag to the ground. Arn, stumbling and bleeding but not spent, tore open the underside of the victim's neck, and it was over—albeit a sloppy and costly hunt.

As they rested after their great feast, Arn began to blame Versa. His side ached as his magnificent coat of silver-gray fur had been torn open. He thought surely the arrogant she-wolf had caused his wounds. What would this mean to him, to survival when wind-driven bitter needles of ice and snow relentlessly pelted him and food grew scarce? Drifting toward sleep, his side oozing and burning, Versa came to his side, licked his wound to cleanse it, and whispered to him, "Never again shall we fail to cooperate, for you and I both must live, if one is to live." He heard her words, which shook him out of his self-pity and need to assess culpability. Then she curled against him protecting his wound, pressing the skin against the muscle to close it, and they slept, especially Arn whose sleep seemed endless. Versa would hold her body against his skin for as long as the other slept, somehow knowing that with time and pressure the wound's healing might be assured. Days passed with Arn sleeping and Versa protecting.

As Arn slept ever so deeply, exhausted by the hunt and the pain of his wound, he dreamed of it and saw something unnoticed in the heat of battle. He saw Versa attempt to knock him down as the buck took deadly aim him. Had she not interceded, the buck's aim would have proved fatal. He also saw his feet first tripping Versa. He awoke and cried a solitary wolf-tear. He felt the guilt of one who realized his failure to trust another most-deserving soul caused by his own self-delusion and ignorance. He felt the guilt of unfairly holding another responsible for his misunderstandings and his own failures. He was then the first wolf to cry. Now wolf-tears are not human tears and are rarer than a four-leaf clover. And wolf dreams are not human dreams. Have you never seen our paws flick and bellies take humorously audible fits? There is much truth seen in wolf dreams. Upon that spot where Arn's tear fell vegetation withered, the earth hardened and cracked, and henceforward no plant has ever grown. Animals will not even pause there, except for venomous creatures when a hot sun warms the desolate slab.

As the season's cold yielded to the rising height of the sun and green shoots were welcomed by the warmth, Arn healed. Versa had provided ample meat and protection while healing came. Arn returned to vigor, a great and powerful wolf, and new behavior was upon him. He was more playful and attentive than ever before. This powerful, immense, ferocious wolf fawned at Versa's feet, chased her in play, and licked her muzzle. Versa, a no-nonsense wolf, put the question to Arn directly: "Why are you being so silly? Where is your wolf pride?" Arn did not answer; he just continued to laud affection upon Versa, which she soon began to appreciate and enjoy.

The lesson was not plain to either, at first. Somehow just like the fish at the streamside, this almost-gone-wrong hunt showed them they needed each other. What would have been undetected because of the savage nature of these wild animals remained a valuable lesson worth remembering. A growing glimmer of loyalty incubated within them, but just a little brighter within Versa. Undetected was the increasing decay of selfishness and need to focus on the faults of the other. So, as they had survived the winter, hunted well together and soon forgot the competition and need for blame, instead they were continuing their education in the first way of the wolf—cooperation.

Though Versa's words represented the most essential part of the Wolf Ways, her purpose was not quite the same as your altruistic self-sacrifice, like a soldier saving comrades by jumping upon a horrible, indiscriminate killing device of war. It is instead the near blindness of the individual wolf to itself. It is the individual's loyalty and commitment to the pack. It is the pursuit of its obligation to the pack ". . . both must live." Unwavering loyalty found in cooperation may be the best description of the first Wolf Way. But like all Wolf Ways, it can be destroyed by the faults and malice of another, purporting to be dedicated to the pack. Because of Arn and Versa, loyalty remains steadfast in the wolf. It is perhaps the greatest tragedy of our new-wolfenness when our now innate loyalty is abused and broken by one of your race.

Do not miss the profound importance of this Wolf Way. The enduring nature and compounded results give testament to its greatness. The Magnificent Ones had discovered that unity is the true essence of their pack existence. All the other Wolf Ways would grow from this necessity. As in the past, they still shape our combined histories; this is why I share our wolf story. For we are clever in our service to each other and to mankind, but we only succeed by using The Wolf Ways lived by The Magnificent Ones, Arn and Versa. And as you will soon learn, taught everywhere by one of their first offspring. Their near-fatal battle and recovery, somehow leading to collaboration had also unknowingly given them a taste of wolf-tolerance. Surely the distance from cooperation to tolerance, to loyalty is not the furthest jaunt.

4

There is much to respect about Arn and Versa: their strength, beauty, intelligence, cleverness, and newfound loyalty. But to respect them as we new-wolves do, you must understand what just happened. Great and independent creatures whose race had lived isolated lives for countless eons were now learning the whole is greater than the sum of its parts. Together we are more than we are apart. And herein lies the essence of the pack. Heady stuff for a wolf, isn't it? You may think so but to us canines it is obvious, and we know much more. But I am getting ahead of myself.

Arn remained playful and attentive for he knew that she had twice saved his life. He knew that she taught him things he did not know. And he certainly never wanted to fight with her again. He also now found her to be beautiful and appealing, irresistible. With his adoration for his beautiful Versa on the rise, Arn began to devote himself to bringing her food and unending attention until he did something no wolf had ever done. Gazing into her eyes he spoke, "Versa, I cannot contain myself any longer. Therefore, I shall dig."

Arn began to dig and dig. Earth, red and brown, sometimes muddy and sometimes dry, dusty and stinky was flying in all directions. Versa could not resist; she started to dig too. Have you not seen one of us new-wolves digging frantically in the earth? Tree roots, no problem. Rocks regardless of size, away with you! They were digging having no idea where they were going but absolutely certain of the urgency to get there.

Together they dug Versa a warm and safe place in the earth where she could rest, for she was now carrying a litter of seven. The first wolf den would be ready well before the end of the nine weeks she carried her litter. No wolf had ever excavated its own den prior; all before had not the commitment to such security for its progeny. No she-wolf had ever carried so many pups and had all of the litter survive. Much was being discovered. Versa beamed at Arn, "What is this place you have created? Why does it appeal to my maternal instincts? I do not know the answers, but I know it shall be good!" Versa jumped in and out of the newly-created den. Filled with excitement, so did Arn. Again and again, they frantically raced in and out of this new place until they both fell to the ground together in wolf-laughter.

For you see, we dig for more than food. We also instinctively dig to protect the new lives we bring into the world.

Remember the first den when you see one of us new-wolves digging up your garden; it is our way for we, too, are wolves. For our race, Arn and Versa performed the first dance of wolf joy. And so it was, Versa, young of years, carried her first litter of seven pups well after the leaves began to dry and scatter. This would be the first of seven litters resulting in seven dens, dug by Arn, each deeper and more spacious than the prior one.

Your ancestors found these great dens, some now filled with stalagmites and stalactites, and with others some of your people even went as far as to build within them. The wisest among you will realize these dens are real and know their locations because of your ancestors. Read on and learn, my dear friends.

While this first wolf pair had learned to hunt together, once fought, saved each other from death, and survived the winter, neither had been part of a parent team before. Nonetheless, they seemed to know what to do. And as the litter of wolf pups came to be born in the den, Versa was the most attentive brood bitch ever known. Seven small, slimy, blind and helpless bundles of life each with its potential, was licked clean, fed well, and kept warm. As Versa cleaned them, licking each in vulnerable spots, at first they all squirmed in resistance. Each had within the instinct to protect its body, but eventually they all submitted to their mother. But two resisted a bit more than all the others. They were also the first, and best, at finding the teat at feeding time and the first to open their eyes.

Versa not only had to feed and clean them, she moved them about the den with her great jaws, grabbing each by the nape of the neck. Using the same tools she had used to save Arn from the great stag—sharp fangs with the potential of immense compression several times of that of your jaws—she now used her powerful jaws to grab her cherished offspring, but with the instinctive gentleness of her maternity. Her instinctive inhibition of her powerful bite reflex when handling such tender ones as these would soon be put to use in wolf-tolerance and eventually in our service to humanity. The inhibited bite, invaluable within the pack and occasionally to outsiders, is one of The Wolf Ways ironically discovered when only isolation and hate ruled over the ancient wolf.

As they feasted on their mother's nutritious milk, Arn brought Versa bits of food, both small and large. Together they had hunted deer, ibex, wild horse, and wild boar. Now hunting alone, he found it easier to bring Versa goat, rabbit, marmot, porcupine, beaver, rat, mole, mouse, and bird. He could not risk injury in the hunt for larger game; he had greater concerns.

Arn never felt quite happy with the new bite-sized menu, so regardless of the required effort, he brought his precious one larger prey whenever he could. Many days he simply said, "My beloved, tomorrow I shall bring you even more bounty.

Please excuse today's meager offering." Of course the meals were not meager, and Versa did not mind any of it.

Even while hunting alone, the things he and Versa had learned together helped him succeed as he performed his commitment to his family, loyalty reinforced with a seven multiple. Sometimes he would lie in the den to keep his children warm as Versa moved about to stretch and exercise her great wolf body and to prepare to embark upon great hunts once again with her unrivaled partner. And he, too, knew how to clean them and how to safely carry them about, and Versa did not fear him or fear for the future of her pups while Arn cared for them. Both Arn and Versa kept their den clean and quickly all their pups learned instinctively never to lie in their own waste.

The pups grew quickly, and as they opened their eyes, Versa began to show them the tunnel out of the den. Squinting, they stumbled into the big world outside with the majestic Arn towering above them in unwavering watchfulness. The days were fresh and the nights were clear and cool. Their den remained warm and safe. Although dark, it gave each growing pup a sense of security. In a place like this very few pups would be lost to stealthy predators, a risk faced by lone wolves. Also, none would now be lost to the inability of their tiny bodies to keep warm and dry, for Arn and Versa had created the wolf den. Many of you have dreams of holidays by a roaring fire, sitting on a stone hearth within a cozy cabin while the snow blankets the field and forest outside. Each one of us, canines and humans, are drawn to the comforts found in our dens.

On such a warm day Arn, filled with gratitude, called out to Versa, "Never has there ever been a better time for any creature upon the earth." Perhaps he was right, for only from such a perfect life and time could the greatness of the wolf pack originate.

She replied, "We prosper upon lush lands. On hills dotted with great forests and divided by cool meadows and clear streams. From the distant mountains to the north and those near us to the east, and upon the plains between, we have dominion over all upon which we gaze." Wolf-life was good.

As the seven grew strong and began to explore the world around the den and beyond, Arn kept watch. No creature, not fox, jackal, weasel, lynx, badger, nor raptor dared to come close to Arn's den and his precious family.

Now you can probably guess what happened next. Arn and Versa began to disagree on how to be the best wolf parents. The little irritating details of their differences began to gnaw at each of them as the pups ventured further from the safety of the den. Arn remembered the dream he had after the near-deadly hunt, and he remembered all that Versa had taught him, especially the invaluable lesson that she whispered in his ear: "For you and I both must live if one is to live."

4

Sensing with his keen wolf nose that Versa, too, was becoming frustrated, he then took his muzzle, and rubbing it against hers, cheek-to-cheek he told his mate, "We shall rule this family together, but for the wolf pups you shall rule, and for the hunt I shall rule. Never is your well-being or authority to be threatened." It was the first time Arn had outwardly spoken the truth of the first of The Wolf Ways. It was only upon this foundation that other Wolf Ways could be built, especially those of tolerance and its indispensable partner, self-control.

Versa looked into his confident gaze. While she, like Arn, had found herself annoyed with the ideas and ways of the other, even over the pups, she knew he was right. Versa softly replied, "Arn, you have spoken wolf-truth. If we are to survive and prosper, we must share and trust each other in these things and more."

And Arn, knowing his beloved was satisfied and fully committed, drew close to Versa gently rubbing her snout with his and said, "I shall live for you with all my heart and all my strength. My devotion to you and our pack shall never diminish as long as my heart beats and longer!"

Thus, they created a division of power and authority based on loyalty, which now inspired devotion. Together they became the alphas. But with it each instinctively retained the right to challenge the other for the good of the pack, but never to fight as before. They were learning not to bite hard when a growl or a nip would suffice. From mutual respect rose an ability for the pair to rule in unison, and in turn, command respect from all others. Now loyalty could exist between the two, and eventually among others, based on the foundation of cooperation, tolerance, and self-control. Suspicion and hostility were being defeated by trust and loyalty.

Nevertheless, packs are funny things. There is a leader, but the leader is open to challenge. In fact, no alpha goes unchallenged. This is how we maintain the strength of the pack. Such a contradiction, don't you think? But of all The Wolf Ways, please remember this great paradox: there must be an alpha or alpha pair, and yet they must be challenged. The challenge is never based on ego or selfishness, but on the necessity that the greatest source of strength, wisdom, and loyalty is always at the helm. All wolves know this and at least some of you know this, too, I hope. While we seldom fight like Arn and Versa did in that famous, momentous battle, we challenge in gentler, yet equally important ways—a stare, a baring of teeth, a dipped head and stiff tail, or simply unwavering persistence.

Perhaps you see this in your pack and in your community, too, although it may make some of you uncomfortable and unfortunately others never notice. But unlike you my dear human friends, we will always instinctively challenge the alphas, for we are wolves. We do not wish everyone to be our friend. We wish everyone to establish their role within our pack or within the next territory. And we require those not of our pack to show us their credentials through subtle cues buried in their behavior and through their scent. Haven't you wondered why we like to sniff you in embarrassing ways? With all living things, our noses can tell us about health, strength or weakness, emotions, and intentions of others. Only now with cooperation, tolerance, loyalty and self-control learned by Arn and Versa could the shared role of the alpha pair in any pack be fully realized and leveraged for good.

5

The radiant heat of the morning sun could not compare to the warmth felt between mother and pup. A small, soft muzzle lay upon the most powerful of wolf snouts, prompting Versa to muse at the tenderness of the moment balanced against the irony of the past. The seven, now growing wiry and agile, began to wrestle each other as all puppies do, to tackle and instinctively wrap their jaws on the necks of their littermates in mock battle. Either Versa or Arn kept watch as the pups pretended to hunt each other, neither as a referee nor as a biased arbiter but always as the protector of their precious family. Occasionally a pup would grab hold of a parent with needle-sharp puppy teeth. This always met with quick and severe retribution for no self-respecting brood bitch or alpha dog allows a puppy to lay its teeth upon them. There is in the wolf pack no allowance for disrespect of the alpha, even in puppy play. This lesson took but once for each of the pups to learn, except for one.

We new-wolves, too, make little distinction between play, hunt, and fight; for we see all in the light of who is alpha. While you may call this disobedience or lack of brainpower and chalk it up to inferior intelligence, it is just a manifestation of our need to rule, to challenge or to dominate for perhaps we may become alpha one day soon. We will follow a strong and smart leader despite our alpha drive, only if deserved. Such a leader shall receive the wolf pack's devotion—a reward of great value not to be abused or squandered. And whether you know or not, there are many ways for us to "lay our teeth" upon you that don't involve our jaws.

Of the seven, one female stood out, the one who resisted most in the den. She did not like her vulnerable underbelly cleaned, and she found being carried by her neck disagreeable. Just a bit quicker, stronger, and more clever than her littermates, Arn and Versa aptly named their daughter Tria. This gifted pup ruled a miniature kingdom and occasionally tested the alphas, in spite of the consequences. Carrying the blue eyes of her dam, even before her entry into wolf maturity she began to dominate her littermates. She pounced on backs and necks, drove her agile body into the sides and hindquarters of the other pups, developing crucial survival skills. She alone inherited her mother's keen eyes, allowing her to detect during the darkest night any movement within the field of her hawk-like gaze. And then there was her nose. Prominent and black, able to read at once dozens of messages in the air, messages about the strength and health of her littermates, messages about what creature lurked about their domain, even at great distances. Her name Tria in wolf-speak means "one who is given three gifts." Besides the gifts of her vision and olfactory senses, she could hear frequencies and low volumes humans cannot. In her, these gifts were superior to all wolves. Many of us new-wolves, however, like to think her three talents represented loyalty, courage, and intelligence.

One other pup, named Jett, also stood apart from the litter. Advanced and agile for his age like Tria, he had about him a unique air of serenity and confidence. Such was his calm demeanor one might think nothing could upset him. Loving to play, this one never seemed to take seriously the little things of puppy existence, unlike Tria who willed only to win. Handsomely rugged and athletic, Jett was the only young wolf that could run with Tria.

At that time certain lone wolves from the outskirts of this perfect part of creation patrolled, prowling along the perimeter of the lands Arn and Versa had made their own. But this kingdom of the first pack was not limited to a fixed place, for as the pups attained young adulthood, they all moved about together in search of food. No other wolf dared challenge The First Wolf Pack or the expanding territory they claimed.

As Arn and Versa together completed one successful hunt after another, taking abundant meals of the finest flesh, many lone wolves soulfully watched, hoping only to scavenge meager remnants. Meanwhile all the members of this first wolf pack grew powerful and became more prosperous. As those lone wolves watched from afar, they became evermore angry and jealous, but the smartest of them also grew a bit curious. Surely this was the great Versa that none could outrun or outfight and the powerful and ferocious Arn whom all feared. How could this unique pair stay together? For this wolf behavior was not seen before Arn and Versa. Before The Magnificent Ones, she-wolves bore pups alone, often in places of poor shelter, where many pups were lost to weasels, lynx, and other predators when the bitch left her brood to hunt.

The lone wolves watched, ever careful to remain at a safe distance as seven pups were now massive and athletic, adolescent wolves—healthy, strong, and clever. Not just clever on their own but clever as a pack. The lone wolves now observed nine wolves hunt together, and helplessly watched the domain of The First Wolf Pack expand across all the hills and valleys east of the great river, all the way to the mountains that welcomed the morning sun, and back to the sea that washed the western shore with eternal waves. They controlled all lands from the rumbling volcano to the south, through the swampy land to the second great valley to the north.

The young wolves hadn't yet earned their places on the front lines during each hunt, but right behind the alphas Tria and Jett ran hard and fast, never far from the action and never tiring no matter the labor. Led by Tria, all her understudies strode close behind Arn and Versa as their hunting skills gained refinement. The lone wolves found themselves pushed further away, their livelihoods diminished, but no lone wolf would yet admit that the wolf pack demonstrated a better way—except for one most curious young male wolf, with beautiful black fur and piercing bright yellow eyes who followed a little closer, especially near the river and hills in the center of Arn and Versa's domain.

Just as Tria's unwavering puppy eyes never missed early lessons from her parents around the den, real world lessons continued unmissed, lessons about the hunt and about the pack. All the pups learned to protect themselves and how to use their incredible senses to predatory advantage.

While busy living this new lifestyle of the wolf pack, Arn and Versa found little time until now to review what they had learned. However, now that their offspring were almost fully grown, their need to constantly focus on pack life subsided.

It was on a day just like any other day Versa looked at Arn and said, "Are you as amazed as I with this crazy, unique life we have created? There are no lone wolves that live like we or that know what we know. What in the world has happened since our misunderstanding?

Arn laughed out loud, "Yes, our misunderstanding!" He moved closer to her and they nuzzled cheek to cheek. He whispered to his beloved mate, "Whatever happened to us does not need a retrospective, what we need is a path forward."

Soon Versa and Arn began to sneak away to discuss all they had learned from their experiences together. With little concern over their brood's safety, and with Tria at the point, their seven gawky teenagers were becoming a formidable gang. Previously, while the pups were young, council could not truly exist. But now with their offspring near full wolf maturity, a private, formal council could be held without interruption at a great distance from their camp.

At the first Wolf Council Arn and Versa established foundational rules. The first was only an alpha could call Council. The second and more obvious rule, no one other than the alphas may participate, unless granted special permission. Any interloper or spy would not be tolerated, for such disrespect would be severely punished by the alphas. As they formalized the Council the Magnificent Ones also deemed it absolutely necessary for the meeting to begin with The Wolf Utterance. It was a sound that expressed the superiority of the alphas in a way that when faintly heard and not understood would nevertheless cut to the quick of the faraway teen wolves. The terrifying yet inspirational sound provoked a combination of fear and reverence. A wolf call to leadership too profound for a young wolf to fully comprehend, it cut and bit down to their very core.

While the alpha's Council met, although their young now had their adult teeth and nearly-adult bodies, Arn always kept his gifted nose and superior eyes on alert just in case they were not yet ready to defend and defeat all. At one such Council, there was a scent in the air, distant and faint, but nevertheless troubling to him. It was the scent of a strong and healthy young male wolf that he had noticed before. The unfamiliar Canine's visits grew increasingly frequent and uncomfortably nearer.

6

As weeks of nearly-perfect days passed, the pack continued to prosper. Although the demands for food kept growing with expanding sizes of the young wolf bodies, Arn and Versa hunted more efficiently than ever. Food was ample and all flourished. Tria and Jett began to hunt closer to the alpha pair, running faster than their siblings and would often be the first to anticipate the perfect angle of the hunt, wishing to push the pack's prey into the jaws of death. Tria would call out to her dear, favorite brother when a hunt commenced, "Jett, we can never be outrun. Let's show the alphas how fast we are!" And Jett would laugh with joy as they outran their siblings, nearly keeping up with Arn and Versa.

Tria also was the quickest to lunge for the neck of the unfortunate objects of the pack's insatiable hunger only after Arn or Versa had completed the ultimate deed. First imitating them with the rag doll shake of small prey and now intensely blood-driven, perhaps Tria was no longer too young for the necks of larger beasts.

Jett and Tria would only play with each other, engaging in mock battles. They always joined the pack's hunt as a subordinate but formidable pair. They had become beta wolves, those for whom the alpha role seemed within reach. Only these two could accelerate enough to be at the alphas' side when hunting's fulfillment occurred. Be it play battle or the hunt, and filled with fight, Tria possessed a spirit that would not quit.

Being aloof to the others, she and Jett often carried on playing alpha pair and holding pretend wolf council hidden from the alphas and their siblings. In one such secret meeting, Tria first shared with Jett her deep knowledge developed from observing their sire and dam.

"Jett, my great brother, I see many things that I must ponder. Do you realize the alphas always know what angle to take for a successful hunt? How is it they always guide us with unwavering discipline without really hurting us with their power? And why do they never bicker or fight with each other? Why do we live together when other wolves live alone? Why do we prosper so?"

This was becoming Tria's obsession—to fully identify and articulate the greatness of the lives lived by Arn and Versa in their establishment and leadership of The First Wolf Pack. Jett loved to listen to his sister explain her observations in glorious detail. Jett pondered in awe how his special sister could explain the things of being a pack wolf to him, and with each play council her accuracy and specificity grew.

"My dear sister," Jett asked. "How is it that you answer each of your questions with such wisdom before I even understand what it is you are asking?" With admiration he continued, "I might think no wolf has ever thought such thoughts as you." And as they ended their play council the two siblings exuberantly raced each other back to the rest of the pack.

As the pack matured Arn and Versa knew much about the messages airborne scents revealed. They knew that young Tria and Jett were maturing faster than the others. They knew these two stood out from the others as they were superior in mind and body. They could smell it! For we wolves know much about our canine friends, enemies, our environment, and our human family through our noses. You have heard how some of my race help our human friends by finding evil things, from harmful substances to medical problems within members of your race. This nose is how we first interpret the things around us. You may use your eyes first to recognize and interpret your surroundings but we, with our very capable noses, know much more about many things than you may realize.

The alphas noticed Tria ignoring her littermates, just as Arn and Versa did when returning from each hunt, shunning enthusiastic greetings for their progeny, eating and then feeding as they chose. Now it was Tria who always insisted on following the alphas. My dear friends, for in the wolf pack it is the alphas who lead the hunt, control socialization, eat first, and are the only ones to mate. Much is the same with us, the new-wolves once the alpha role is firmly established and enforced.

Arn chuckled to Versa, "Our daughter is becoming much like you, my beloved. She quite reminds me of you as she leads the others of the pack with her speed and strength. And she shows acute awareness, cleverness on the hunt, and now her recent displays of leadership really set her apart."

Versa smiled in amused agreement, recollecting how she first knew Tria was special when one of the male pups, Fic, challenged her over a bony remnant of the pack's feasts. First, Tria showed wide her teeth to Fic, warning him to stay away. Fic, rejecting his sister's warning veered sideways, attempting to put his body closer to the marrow-laden prize. In the blink of an eye with incredible speed and strength Tria took Fic down, propelling the most solid strength of her chest like a bludgeon into his side while taking his neck into her jaws, throwing him to ground and forcing him onto his back. Almost instantly, Fic pressed all four of his legs against Tria in resistance but then after brief hesitation relaxed them in submission.

Tria had asserted herself like the alphas had done whenever an overly-enthusiastic pup put its teeth upon them. For the teeth of the subordinates will never be tolerated by any self-respecting alpha wolf. While growing, the pups learned about the wolf warning smile after just one lesson. None ever again challenged the alphas, but Fic was unwilling to acknowledge this communication from one of his siblings. So Tria did what she had learned from Arn and Versa, to assert her dominance for she was the greatest of her generation. Soon giving in, Fic did just what he had learned to do as a blind pup, to submit his vulnerable belly to a dominant member of the pack.

Jett watched his beloved sister and amiable brother, laughing in curious delight. He called out to her, "Tria, he is your brother, a member of our pack, don't be so uptight." And Jett chuckled again as he watched Tria angrily crushing the bone with her jaws as Fic dusted himself off and moved on to another, smaller and less appealing bone.

7

The innocent contemplation of snow by children and pups is a glorious experience. It is a source of joy and pure pleasure to understand the profound beauty of nature. And for some it remains within their hearts for a lifetime. Living in the moment at such times, a distant memory of our primeval spirit seems to come forth as an outpouring of delight over simple things, things of our Mother Earth for whom we wolves are devoted and grateful. These things are us and we are they.

With the first snowfall Arn was again transformed into the wolf that playfully and adoringly fawned over Versa. And his pups, too, were transformed, even Tria the big-boss-want-to-be could not resist. Leaping and pouncing, running and sliding even fallen sticks from the now bare trees became precious toys of a mock hunt. Versa's heart soared. She thought of how far she and Arn had come. Now dominating the landscape in all directions, with seven healthy pups reaching adult size in time for winter, Versa thought of the things she and Arn had discovered together, knowing they were good. Looking into Arn's eyes Versa queried rhetorically: "What started out as an accidental joint hunt, then shortly afterward a battle of near complete destruction has somehow become this idyllic life? How is this possible?"

Arn remained silent as he felt immersed in satisfaction and happiness. Versa and he realized that their ways were new and unique. They lived as the alpha pair, knew the wind and vectors, lived out cooperation, tolerance and loyalty, established the den, and the showing of teeth.

In the wonders of pack life that day, they watched as Fic approached Tria with his ears back and tail flat, showing submission, and she allowed him to greet her with a stick, which he dropped at her feet. Tria turned, Fic followed, and she allowed him to do so after a piercing stare held him at bay for more than a moment. She then found a place of shelter under a pine tree and lay down near where Jett had perched to watch the sibling conflict. Fic followed closely and laid beside her. Jett also ignored him. Arn and Versa settled down too, and the others found places near them. All was right in their world.

On the occasion of the season's first snowfall, as dusk settled upon them the pups knew young wolf joy. Sleeping deeply, they dreamed wolf dreams of hunting and feasting, of play, and of the joy of the pack. In contrast, Arn found his sleep haunted by knowledge of a troublesome lone wolf. The obvious scent of the stranger with black fur and piercing bright yellow eyes did not interfere with Versa's sleep, but Tria slept restlessly. Thoughts of concern for his pack consumed Arn's interrupted sleep. Filled with agitation, his rest was replaced by a mysterious anxiety of spirit. With this his ire grew.

He recognized the maturing Tria would soon become a she-wolf. He could smell the changes about her. Her size and strength were approaching Versa's. Her speed and her cleverness surpassed the other pups. And she had the beginning of the smell of things just like the day Arn began to dig in his first dance of wolf joy, when earth flew and his body ached for Versa. He arose, while all others slept. Arn moved slowly into the breeze that carried the scent of a lone wolf, studying it with great discernment, being ever so quiet, as silent as a peregrine before its dive, soaring on a thermal updraft over a sunbaked landscape. For the lone wolf did not know the lesson Versa had taught Arn about understanding and using the direction of the wind. He only knew of times when his hunger ached for the taste of creatures that he could not take.

He had been curious for a long while to know why The Magnificent Ones stayed together and why they flourished so. At times, there was another new and faint scent that wafted about him that drove him closer to the first pack even when his aching stomach caused him the greatest suffering.

On this day, driven by the smell of the first pack's most recent feast and more, the intruder named Bord fell into the trap of Arn's knowledge and cunning.

You already know that no wolf before had Arn's size and strength, so it did not take but a moment for him to dispatch the hungry invader. Surprised by Arn from a secret corner of the forest, Bord had nowhere to run as Arn attacked. Taking place within the range of Versa's senses, she caught the scent of wolf blood up for the battle, like confrontation smelled the days of their epic fight. Versa sprung to her feet and with incredible speed raced to the scene of Arn's domination.

As Bord attempted to protect himself from the greatest of all wolves, he was driven onto his back, into the jagged rocks between two trees and finding his adversary an irresistible agent of death. Defensively he used all the strength in his legs to attempt to keep Arn at bay as Versa arrived. At the moment of Arn's intent to vanquish him, Bord instinctively released the resistance of his legs and submitted just as a puppy being cleaned by its mother must do. Versa, throwing herself into the one-sided fight, prevented Arn from applying the deadly blow as Bord surrendered. Bord whimpered as Versa took her turn grabbing the exposed neck of this stranger, while Arn stepped back. He had just inhibited his bite and let Bord live.

Now in any other time before The First Wolf Pack, the intruder would have met with an immediate and unforgiving execution. But not when the first alpha pair was at work. The First Wolf Pack developed the inhibited bite, the ability to mitigate the power within their jaws of death and communicate to others without severe damage. You may know this technique as the sting and bruise of a dog's nip. But I hope you never experience the power of a real dog bite; this is usually reserved for fights of survival and for predatory acts. It has many times the power of the nip. Applied in vulnerable places a single bite can easily be fatal, even to beasts of your size. Fortunately for Bord, the inhibited bite stemming from the discovery of tolerance and discernment saved him from destruction by Arn.

As Arn and Versa stood down, the stay of execution granted, Bord groveled. Arn demanded "Why do you keep us under reconnaissance?"

The thin young wolf mustered the strength to answer the powerful pair with honesty. "I am very hungry and jealous of your success. And I want to know why you all run together; are you not wolves?"

Versa whispered in Arn's ear "I smell a simple and honest heart on this one. He means us no harm. We have ample food and his handsomeness reminds me a little bit of you."

A bit incredulous at Versa's comparison, Arn called to the scrawny but handsome one. "This way thin one; today you may live." Bord followed as close as the alpha pair would allow.

Returning to their pack, Arn and Versa found seven near-adult wolves in a circle, agitated and ready for battle with Tria at the point, looking more menacing than they had seen before. The young wolves instinctively knew from the messages in the air there had been a threat to their pack. Now this means everything to the future of the wolf pack, for Arn and Versa had been teaching them the first lesson of the wolf pack. As Bord moved closer, Tria, with Jett coming to her side led the way and boldly approached him. Showing her teeth, Bord passively submitted to her by rolling over and exposing himself to evisceration. Tria snapped at him, then took a long sniff, only allowing him to get back to his feet when she felt satisfied with her exhibition of dominance.

Versa recognized that this hungry young wolf was perhaps only six full moons older than her litter. While quite thin, he was otherwise healthy and very athletic. His sparkling eyes and shabby fur were mounted on a frame that somewhat resembled a smaller version of Arn. Versa then allowed Jett to take him to the remnants of yesterday's kill. Tria waited impatiently for Jett to complete the act of hospitality so they could sneak off for one of their special play councils to review and discuss what had just occurred.

As their amateur meeting began, Jett saw in Tria a new wolf emotion; it was a burning desire for the annihilation of another wolf. He asked her: "Why do you see this new one as a threat to us? Surely the alphas know what is right, do they not?" Jett tried to get her to focus on the discovery of the inhibited bite and the wolf-tolerance the alphas had shown to the intruder, but she could only speak of how differently she would have handled the event.

"Outsiders must not be allowed," she repeated again and again.

Eventually, at Jett's persistence, Tria turned her focus to her brother's interest in the topic of tolerance, but unlike other times, she had little to say. He sloughed off his sister's hostility as a strong desire to protect the pack. It made much sense to Jett since Tria had talked of these two Wolf Ways in the past.

For weeks, as Bord was allowed to stay with The First Wolf Pack, Tria struggled to contain her animosity. Often in restless dreams she would attack him and successfully correct the mistake of the alphas. But to Tria and the others it did not appear the alphas had accepted him in a way that seemed permanent.

8

The two Magnificent Ones, seven of their nearly-perfect offspring, and Bord—the adopted older cousin to the pups—were on the move, gaining territory further into the mountains to the east of their original land, including smaller hills, valleys, swampland, and a river. They feasted on other, newly-discovered creatures at will.

All of the pack followed Arn and Versa on the hunt, taking the alpha's lead at all times. Even though winter was upon the high country to the east, the bountiful fur of each wolf in the first pack kept them warm when they hunted there. And in the depth of the coldest nights if Arn and Versa allowed, the pack huddled together for warmth as the alphas had done during their first winter together—just like the time when Arn dreamed and Versa whispered.

As young Bord became an effective part of the hunting machine, he began to forget the severe aching in his belly that formed the center of his previous existence. In his well-fed and youthful enthusiasm for being admitted to the pack he tried to initiate play with others but usually endured the rejection of a tackle by the neck or wolf grin—the baring of teeth. Sometimes the young wolves mounted him—just as your own dog might do to your leg or that of a visitor—to show dominance not sexual desire.

But Bord did not care, rolling onto his back in submission whenever necessary to avoid a fight and waiting for his superiors to initiate play. Regularly, he suffered Arn's or Versa's ire, who seemed to target only him for torment. Sometimes Tria treated him most cruelly of all.

Despite his now impressive size, Bord found himself still the omega wolf, the last one of the pack, the wolf at the bottom who served as the alphas' tool for exhibiting pack discipline, showing their power through occasional brutality. He ate last, received greetings last, and might not ever mate, yet his existence seemed most excellent nonetheless.

Irrespective of his omega role, the entire pack listened in rapt attention when Bord told stories of how word spread among the lone wolves of Arn and Versa's marauding wolf pack, their ownership of a vast hunting territory, and the birthing cave near one of the majestic hills near the great stream. He also spoke of a massive and charismatic lone wolf, who was a bit older than all the others but nonetheless dominant, surviving by incredible cunning and viciousness.

Many other wolves found themselves lulled into a false sense of security when he turned on the charisma, soon to lose its meal or its life, or both. This lone wolf he feared more than all others was none other than his own sire, Ket the Elder. On the day Bord first encountered Arn, pinned between the rocks, he thought his attacker might be that lone wolf which all others feared most.

Bord explained, "Ket the Elder is the only wolf who might be capable in size and strength to challenge Arn or Versa in a one-on-one battle." At this the pack jeered him for speaking such nonsense.

Arn interrupted his youngsters, however, saying, "Bord, before Versa and I became one, I battled with this one you say is almost my match. He attempted to steal a wild goat I had taken by chasing several young deer directly in front of me just as I had completed my taking of the beast. I rose to chase the frightened deer, not being able to resist the hunt and such bounty. But as the smell of the goat was still strong within my nose, I halted and turned only to see this one you call Ket attempting to carry off my original kill."

All of the pack shouted, demanding to know what happened. Arn, having wolf-timing paused just long enough to build suspense then continued, "I accelerated toward the thief and propelled my body into him like a colossal boulder crashing down a cliffside. As the force of my body struck him, I felt as if I had collided with a mighty oak, so strong was he. Both stunned, we each regrouped and grabbed the goat carcass to claim it. As we tugged, he was able to rip apart a full hindquarter. And then he trotted off. There was much power in his jaws, neck and chest, which I could feel as he stole the ration. I swear I could hear a snicker as he dashed into the woods."

Hearing these stories, much suspicion brewed inside Tria. She thought this one called Bord, like his sire, might be using guile to play the omega wolf. Engendering their trust, he gained strength, size, and skill from the pack, while hiding his nefarious purpose—spying.

Jett and Fic, however, befriended this interloper and showed no concern. Sometimes Jett and Fic allowed Bord to join in a game of wolf-tag, running down one another by grabbing one another's legs while in full sprint and wrestling the opponents to the ground. While often the prey in this game, the intense exercise helped Bord grow tough and nimble of foot, with all of them benefiting by learning how to take down larger prey. Sometimes Fic allowed Bord to chase him, which made Tria very angry.

To understand Bord, let us return to our origins, to the time of the lone wolf. Mature females only permitted superior male wolves to approach when the urgings of nature visited; the need to reproduce blinded both sexes to their suspicion of all other wolves. They mated and then parted company only to perhaps fight with each other in the season that followed, competing for food and full of suspicion. And some, like Bord as the omega wolf, might never know the reproductive culmination of their nature.

Except for only the greatest specimens of canine power, the lives of all lone wolves remained meager, filled with hunger and conflict. For untold centuries, many died from hunger or from injuries received in battles with other wolves or with their quarry. The litters were small, and only one or two pups might survive their first year. The father of a young wolf might sometimes be its slayer knowing, but not caring, that the blood of its victim was the same blood coursing through its own veins.

Now why would two creatures as vicious as Arn and Versa let one battle change their entire nature? What miraculous source inspired these two alphas to create The First Wolf Pack? Although legend does not offer these details, the greatness of this event remains clear.

Not only did Arn and Versa remain paired season after season, they also broke the hate-filled instincts of the lone wolf by allowing their young adult progeny to serve as part of The First Wolf Pack and by allowing Bord to join them. The pack subsequently discovered and cultivated deeper virtues, such as wolf-gratitude, which history credits to Bord and which only very wise creatures, like the canines and humans, could learn.

For this pack learned to suppress the indiscriminate drive to kill others of their own species and learned to submit to qualified leaders and cooperate for the good of the pack. For Bord, how could he not discover gratitude? He went from emaciated, flea-infested, paltry survival to acceptance into a life of protected, shared wolf opulence. Bord grew strong, wise, and loyal.

In the prior, dark time of the lone wolf, it was not always the smartest or the strongest that survived. Survival also depended on other factors. Perhaps a strong and healthy male wolf, exhausted by a successful hunt would be ambushed by another wolf or by a bear. Without the pack to provide defense, the great creature would not have the chance to improve his race when bitches were in season. Truly in that early time my ancestors scratched out a barren, meager existence.

But a potential wolf revolution visited our race—sire, dam, offspring, and one outsider stayed together. Hunting together, huddling together, protecting each from all threats, and following the alphas, contributed to the advancement of my race.

When Bord stalked The First Wolf Pack, he was driven by hunger and the smell of Tria. But a full belly would have to satisfy the cravings of his nature, for he could not stand up to the alphas, nor to his adopted siblings, especially Tria. Though he began to exhibit loyalty as much as any other member of The First Wolf Pack, some remained unable to see his virtue.

She would not have him and might have fulfilled her restless, murderous dreams, but Jett had unconditionally accepted the outsider. Like a drill sergeant who had successfully completed training with a crack unit, once demanding and hostile, Jett was now willing to show acceptance and more. This was all that kept Tria from an act of slaughter.

Jett, the Pack's first born now displayed a fine physique, intelligence, personal allure, and alpha potential. His prowess grew from the physical and mental demands of the hunts and games of wolf-tag, supplemented with nourishment from the great shared feasts of the hunting machine. His stature and his molten-yellow eyes were the image of a young Arn. But as Jett matured, his blood began to boil with lust, which inevitably would soon blind him to his submissive role in the pack. Arn and Versa knew he must leave. If not this year, perhaps the very next season would find him challenging the great Arn for dominance.

Today Jett was not wolf enough, yet still too much wolf to stay. The importance of this event cannot be overstated. Arn could have killed his son if challenged then and there, but that would be inconsistent with the newly-learned wolf-tolerance. So, he decided to drive the young Jett from the pack. Only one male could rule.

Arn knew what he had to do. In a most aggressive posture he slowly, while staring daggers, walked directly up to Jett. He showed his teeth while maintaining his stare. A growl emanated from Arn, loud and guttural. Jett tried to retreat. Arn sprang into action, bounding into Jett's side and nipping him hard on his side, right above his foreleg. Jett spun toward Arn in a mock attempt to defend himself. This time Arn hit him hard with a bite to Jett's ear, grabbing it as if it were prey. Once released, Jett stepped back several feet and showed his teeth, but then looked away. This time Arn launched himself at Jett, causing the young wolf to run. Arn faked another attack, snarling and snapping, yet left his son unharmed. Jett understood the message—stay and fight for control or depart. Although young, Jett had enough wolf-sense not to stand and fight.

Versa, standing near the action to complete the alpha pair, spoke: "Jett, you are a most powerful and capable wolf. We banish you from the pack, not as an enemy, but as one too strong to stay. With this strength you must find a she-wolf equal to your capabilities and begin the second wolf pack. It is time for you to leave."

Jett knew he had received excellent preparation for this moment. He possessed all essential physical attributes and the intellectual savvy of his wise and gifted parents. He also enjoyed a truly unique advantage—Tria's private instruction, each lesson indelibly etched in Jett's mind.

Now banished, Jett was the first to venture from The First Wolf Pack, not with the limitations of the lone wolf but with the knowledge of using the wind, understanding direction and speed together, along with the near-perfect body replica of Arn. At two winters old his ego and ear barely bruised, he trotted out of the pack carrying the confidence of youth, ready for adventure, giving little thought to leaving his beloved sister Tria and the others behind.

Believing as do the teens of your race, he knew all he needed to know to chart his own course. Arn and Versa silently mourned that they would never hunt with him again. His amiable nature, discernment, and his hunting skills made him very special in their eyes. And they were also saddened to think he would not enjoy the teamwork of many hunts with Tria, with whom they knew Jett had a special bond. Truly these two had developed pair-hunting skills to nearly rival Arn and Versa, but alone how successfully would he hunt?

With generations of lone wolf blood still in his veins he sprinted up the side of a hill on a luscious spring morning while Tria watched in despair. Now out of sight of The First Wolf Pack, stopping upon the crest Jett gazed out over other lands on the edge of the domain of The Magnificent Ones. Instantly, Jett knew that he had journeyed into this world precisely for this day.

Under his cold stare he saw two lone wolves locked in battle over the mutilated body of a young swine, for each had attacked the unfortunate creature simultaneously, from opposite sides. The plump prize now forgotten to the battle, he curiously watched what he had only experienced in play. His keen nose knew from the scent in the air this was the type of lone wolf battle Versa had spoken of during the stories of wolf wisdom shared while the pack rested after each feast born of successful hunts. He recalled her brilliant explanation of the inhibited bite for the sake of life without deadly battles, and for just a moment, he missed his pack. He wondered why the two lone wolves would not simple share the fat prize as would his pack—it was more than ample in its fleshy abundance.

Snapped back to the reality of the carnage occurring in front of him by the sound of a lone wolf cry that he knew was death's morbid song, one wolf shuddered and fell, jerked and went silent. Born of greatness Jett's confidence and curiosity propelled him to the scene. There he found a she-wolf standing over the body of the vanquished. Barely harmed herself she licked her foreleg where a small trickle of blood persisted. As Jett approached nearer, she charged him, willing to defend her meal even against a second, larger villain. As she neared, Jett cocked all four legs and released his body like a single bolt of lightning propelling his chest into this young she-wolf as he had first seen Tria do to Fic. Bowling her to the ground almost at the spot where the porcine carcass lay, he took her lean throat in his jaws but resisted his impulse to kill, instead using the inhibited bite. She was tougher than her thin frame might imply, and Jett held her this way until she ceased resisting. It wasn't until the next afternoon that she stood on her four legs again.

Jett pondered this impressive young she-wolf's vitality and courage, and he felt quite satisfied with himself for not executing her. In a way, Jett thought, her incredible will to fight, to resist—even against his superior power—reminded him of Tria, the one who did not quit, the member of his generation who showed the most tenacity and determination. He considered that although Tria inherited slightly more of these two gifts, he received a calmness of heart his sister didn't possess. Satisfied with the distribution of personality gifts, Jett felt a longing for hunts and play council with his sister as he spent many hours holding down this beautiful little stranger despite her struggles to escape. With both a mortally-wounded swine and the carcass of the vanquished wolf there upon the little battlefield, a few lone wolves began to approach, but seeing Jett so dominant—looking like the great Arn himself—none had the fortitude to attempt to steal the tempting meal. Finally released, the once victor turned subordinate returned to her original intention. She even had the courage and audacity to turn her back to Jett as she proceeded to gorge herself.

9

Perhaps in no other being is the will to survive greater than in the wolf. Essential to the survival of the lone wolves and continuing through to the prospering of The First Wolf Pack was the pure tenacity that lay at the core of their nature. It was through the teaching of The Magnificent Ones that persistence was tempered and thus perfected. Blind, persistent suspicion, after all, was part of what doomed countless generations of my ancestors to paltry lives. Fortunately, the unremitting will to survive prevented their extinction.

Jett recalled Tria's explanation of how Arn and Versa discovered that persistence required a sister who they knew as discernment, and how they discovered that their decisions based on a life dedicated to each other provided them with much more than the individual gave up. Tria once said to Jett, "Our parents were the first to discover that at times, a growl proves superior to a bite." In contrast, they also knew when to apply their unrelenting determination to battle, to the hunt, and to leadership.

Jett found no doubt or flaw in this lesson. That is why he let Ellip live. As she ceased her futile struggle against Jett's incredible power, he let her get to her feet, stepped back, and turned his back on her and the now fly-covered swine. Ellip dove to her prize of two different battles and hastily ate while Jett turned momentarily to watch, then he trotted off slowly with the breeze at his back, his nose knowing all the while that soon he would have a companion. With a barely perceptible limp from her bleeding foreleg, Ellip soon bounded after Jett, enamored with curiosity and something she had not felt before, respect.

He called to her, "What is it you seek by following me?"

Ellip replied in a sarcastic way that greatly amused Jett, "I will let you know if you do something noteworthy."

Let me interrupt the story to tell you here that what you call love is not as powerful in our pack as is respect. The love you place upon us like primates with hugs and kisses we tolerate, and some of us enjoy it more than others, but it is not what drives us to loyalty.

That afternoon as Ellip came closer to Jett, he stopped, turned, and stared at her until she froze in her tracks, lowered her head and neck in a cowering posture not daring to make eye contact, and approached slowly. Then when within only a few feet from Jett, she turned and came to him sideways, not face-to-face, which is often a sign of aggression. Having only known the way of the lone wolf it is a mystery to us that she submitted to him in both battle and in approach. While Bord first submitted to the great Arn like a puppy, and then learned from The Magnificent One's pack the ways of regularly showing submission to the alpha, Ellip had no knowledge of adult submissive behavior. Perhaps she was one of the lone wolves observing the pack from a distance. Our legend does not tell us why, but we do know that her act of submission lurked within her nonetheless; for without it, Jett would not have allowed her to live long enough to join him. But live she did.

I've always wondered about Ellip's scent and gait. What was it about her that caused Jett to teach her instead of dispatching her and devouring her hard-earned meal? Perhaps it was the way she conquered her adversary at the porcine battle, or perhaps something else. Certainly, her sarcastic quip appealed to his sense of humor. But I know she must have been more unique and gifted than our legend describes because Jett allowed her to follow him for another day, mostly at a short distance. He then grew hungry. Turning into the wind and raising his great nose high, he found delight in the messages of the air. Changing direction, he ran off at three-quarter speed with Ellip at his left keeping pace. She seemed to know that something exciting was upon them.

Ellip called out to Jett, "I shall follow you at any speed for you are no typical wolf!"

He laughed in reply saying, "Nor are you my beautiful and tenacious friend. Let us see how quickly you might learn." And they began to move as one.

Breaking into a thicket and slowing from movement to stillness in an instant, Jett froze near the edge of the under-brush. He then carefully inched forward until ready to break the woody barrier. Suddenly he burst into a squawking argument of fat geese. Instinctively Ellip followed Jett's every move faultlessly. It reminded him how he and Tria always worked in perfect harmony.

They leaped from the thorny lair. All but two of the migrants found lift under their broad wings, while each wolf easily laid fangs upon the failed take-offs of feathers and lean meat. Then the wolf pair ate, each their own bird, but there was no suspicion. Jett laughed in amusement as he watched Ellip, feathers protruding from her mouth, struggle with how to eat such a meal. Naturally wise, she stopped her feathered struggles and looked to him as he continued his cleaning of the bird, and she imitated his technique.

Remember how lone wolves ever-stalked their hated brethren? During and after the first hunt, these two new companions knew no hate. Jett radiated *joie de vivre*, which Ellip saw fit to emulate. And Ellip enjoyed fowl, which she had never before eaten. Geese's and other fowl's heightened sense of hearing made it challenging for lone wolves to successfully take them down, and as yet, Ellip had no knowledge of wind or stealth.

Certainly, it was the leadership that exuded from Jett that subdued her will to ambush him once freed and now in the hunting. The wisdom of her decision was confirmed. He led her into the wind the next morning, and they found a volume of the freshest of meat beyond her prior experience. Deer, fleet of foot and moving with all defensive senses operating, were startled to find two wolves working together outside of the valleys of The Magnificent Ones. Startled too late was the one creature that would fill Ellip's belly beyond anything she had known, for not only did she feast, she had no fear of theft as no lone wolf thief dared approach as she reclined at Jett's table.

Prosperity introduced itself to Ellip through Jett's leadership and tolerance. As they began to hunt together Jett showed her The Wolf Ways he had learned well from the example of the alphas and the dazzling play councils with Tria. Ellip comprehended and seemed to expand upon their success with her uniquely gifted ways. Now permanently paired with Jett, she became even more beautiful, wise, and powerful. Soon she experienced her second season. Jett danced with wolf joy in anticipation of their first litter.

Jett began calling with soulful howls into the brisk night sky, frosted breath gathering under the moonlight in small twinkling clouds. His first offerings to the night consisted of gratitude for life's good fortune. Just as Arn and Versa each pondered the prosperity of the pack the summer after the first litter was weaned, Jett's profound comprehension derived from both the perspective of pup and now as an alpha. His songs reached far across the dotted valleys and into the range of Tria's great ears. Joyfully she realized this meant her brother had now achieved Arn's dream for Jett. No wolf had ever before sung into the night with wolf-speak, which you humans foolishly call howling.

10

Jett, Tria's perfect student, somehow moved by a deep need to share with the companions of his youth burst out in wolf song never heard before. His great lungs and powerful thorax produced melodious strains of a soulful and lyrical sincerity. Without guarantee that any canine would understand his song, the new alpha's grand tenor first honored those who raised him. Jett's voice rang out in gratitude for his great success. Next, he revealed the glorious details of his progeny, born of his incomparable mate, whose cleverness, loveliness, and tenacity made his life complete.

The ways of Arn and Versa did not contemplate topics shared over great distances. Hearing the distant wolf sounds, they immediately recognized the voice of their first born, Jett. But they did not understand the meaning or purpose, only somehow sensing the emotions. It was only Tria who could understand all. As she listened intently to Jett, trying to comprehend each new sound, Tria contemplated how this new communication might enhance the invaluable gifts of The Magnificent Ones.

As she listened, Tria understood: "Grateful am I to be born of Arn and Versa. Grateful am I for Ellip, blessed that I should enjoy such beauty and bounty in my life." He repeated his message night after night. He always ended his songs with a special message: "Tria, you are my gifted and brilliant sister. I know someday you will have all the blessings of The First Wolf Pack and much more."

As his songs continued week after week, he spoke across the stillness of the night with reports of their recent successes, always with thanks given to his now distant benefactors. And always at the end of each song, he sent a message for his special sister, Tria. Jett hoped that someday she would learn to interpret these sounds, thus adding wolf songs to her repertoire and genius. He did not yet know that she had understood every message from his very first song.

While all lone wolves too heard this new night-filling sound, only the pack of The Magnificent Ones, led by Tria, tried to understand. But with her understanding of his messages, she selfishly wondered why Jett had to leave her and why he had the joy that eluded her?

Of course, it was Tria who first deciphered Jett's ballads, for she and her brother were always of the same mind. Suppressing her festering loneliness caused by the absent Jett,

Tria decided to offer her interpretation of his songs to all the others in the pack.

Nights passed and all the others found it difficult to imitate Jett's new vocalizations although some tried. Failing to understand his communication had very specific meaning, like your human way of speaking, only gibberish stumbled from their throats. Wolves and we new-wolves do not have complex devices in our throats to make unlimited and unique utterances as do you, making the babble that emanated from them all the more ridiculous.

Now fully mature, the powerful and clever Tria, having gained complete mastery of The Wolf Ways quickly recognized that while all knew the singer, none knew the song except for herself. Thus, knowing how special she was in all ways and realizing she alone understood Jett, she approached Versa and flatly stated the need for a Wolf Council.

"My alphas, I have understood my brother's song, which you and the others have not. I have observed your ways of success, and I have cataloged them, which you and the others have not. Let us meet in Council, and I shall teach you what you do not know."

Tria had been articulating The Wolf Ways to Jett and had known for some time that her parents held special time alone. Therefore, why should not she, in her mind the greatest of their offspring, be entitled to participate? She and Jett had heard their hints at "Council" with their clever snickers at their inside joke, their private secret. Undoubtedly Tria knew—for like Arn her nose could smell the intent of others and her ears could hear the faintest whispers even while she nested with her siblings—that such a thing called Wolf Council existed. And she had led many play councils. But she never shared her suspicions with anyone except Jett until she stood up to Versa that day to demand Council, and it was at that moment that she was banished from the pack.

Her mother imparted a cold and deadly stare that coursed with poisoned blood, never blinking while her chest expanded, her tail dropped flat and stiff, and her ears went forward. Prior to this moment Tria had not seen such wolf hatred directed at anyone, except only mildly toward Bord. And never before did it scare her, for never was it so genuine of Versa's greatness. The scent of Versa's dominance filled the air between them like a freshly-slaughtered skunk. For a moment, Tria thought she should fight as the two held their hateful glares at each other. But fear being the emotional victor this time, insecure in her youth, Tria blinked first then looked away in submission.

11

As Jett before her, Tria trotted away from her home, but this time a wolf-tear dropped to the earth. It landed on the same bare spot upon which Arn had shed the first-ever wolf-tear. We new-wolves know that on this spot no life of any kind has ever since emerged for so great was her loss, her feelings of confusion and betrayal amplifying ten-fold that spot of Arn's tear of guilt. With this spot holding Arn's painful realization that he might have killed the one who would save him, the desolation of this spot now expanded with the wolf-tear of one truly alone, unappreciated, and banished from her home for wanting to do good. The smell of Versa's domination stuck in her great olfactory glands and would not dissipate as Tria sulked away from the only home she had ever known.

Only one generation of suspicion and blood lust removed, this offspring of The Magnificent Ones bore a heart of togetherness and pure dedication to their pack. But it was only as a thin layer covering over the ancient and poisoned blood of the lone wolf. While her intent in calling for Council was to inform and enlighten, she was not entitled to do so. After all of her learning about The Wolf Ways, her understanding of the paramount importance of the alpha role was not complete. Tria had much to share but not the emotional maturity and judgment to bide her time or change her tactics. Unlike Jett who left with optimism, Tria left empty-hearted but physically and intellectually more well-prepared for success than any other could. She had best learned all The Wolf Ways plus she had been the first to understand Jett's long-distance communication.

With her head in an emotional swirl at hearing Jett's song, and not exactly knowing what had just occurred there, Tria simply thought it logical that a Council with the alphas should include her. There she would explain her deep intellectual understanding, explaining how she had cataloged The Wolf Ways and now also knew how to interpret Jett's messages.

She had hoped to teach the others how to fully understand The Wolf Ways and how to learn the new language, but demanding a Wolf Council was exclusively the domain of the alphas. Certainly, her demand conveyed insubordination. The threat made to an alpha wolf by stepping outside one's role is never a good idea. Alas, no lesson would be taught to the alphas that day by the only one who understood what was cried aloft into the ancient wind.

And as Tria trudged off toward a small and distant hill, she heard Jett speak of many lone wolves in her direction. It was then she knew she was not alone. Tria's trot turned into a sprint that carried her far without exhaustion for she sprung from the one none could outrun. She ran not in the direction of Jett's songs, but into an empty blackening nightfall. Tria sought solitude in the emptiness before her since with Jett she would find the pain of jealousy and the pack would only reject her.

Ascending to the top of another hill she slowed at the crest. Distracted by a tiny light just in front of her, Tria stopped. The light fluttered in front of her, but she resisted the instinct to snap her powerful jaws. Instead she cocked her head to adjust her keen ears. A sweet, soft, song-like buzz emanated from the source of the pleasing light. Intrigued, Tria settled her great wolf body into the comfortable grass to watch and try to understand this new thing. As her sit reclined into laying, the appealing light approached her with a grand vista behind; she felt no threat but instead a faint glimmer of happiness began to build in the recently banished one's heart.

The small light settled on her great forepaw and rested upon her lavish fur. Tria moved her muzzle to smell this thing and it emitted two quick, soft pulses of light, then it spoke in the softest voice ever spoken and that only the great wolf's ears could hear.

"Thank you for not eating me or squashing me with your mighty paw, my princess."

Tria understood her words but wondered how this creature knew wolf-speak. Then the mighty wolf spoke to this tiny creature with attempted gentleness but her powerful lungs blasted the little one deeply into her fur.

"What is your name?"

No answer.

"Why do you glow like nothing else?"

No answer. Then the little one elevated into the evening sky and began to glow again, more intensely than before. Suddenly springing from the shelter of the grasses of the downslope of Tria's perch, a thousand identical small lights arose, blinking and singing an impossibly-soft song that filled the young she-wolf with immense pleasure. The sky was alive with joy.

She repeated her demand of the little one as it came close to her again, "Who are you?"

This time the tiny creature spoke; "We are The Last. I am called Joy."

Tria again pursued, "Why do you glow like no other creature?" But no answer came. Joy simply joined the others as they sang and gently shone a heart-lifting display.

Tria realized at that moment that the profound sadness of banishment had retreated and her spirit was fortified. With a calm spirit she walked a short way into a stand of carob and holly oak trees against a small cliffside where ancient rains had washed away soil and rock exposing the compacted skeletons of earlier ages. With a view to most of the land before her and a soft sheltered place on which to lie, she settled down to rest, now somewhat at peace. Tria's grand nose set directly into the wind and with ears erect, nothing could approach her without her knowledge. For only her ears could hear and understand Jett's messages as well as Joy's soft song; they, too, could hear the approach of a tiny spider at the length of a wolf's stride. And her nose set to the wind could smell all things near and far, distinguishing all from the other, knowing each creature and its place in her new domain. Soon asleep, Tria dreamed of warm summer days playing with Jett in mock battles and she dreamed of grand hunts where the pack took all the nourishment it sought. These dreams of pack life also comforted her.

Awakening to the first note of the first song of the first bird who beckons farewell to the night sky before the morning sun illuminates the eastern horizon, Tria rose. She stretched her great wolf body like the bow of play we new-wolves do to entice your interest, then also stretched her hind legs in full extension, one after the other. This day would not be like

the last. And in the rich fur of her foreleg, she observed Joy
nestled and still.

12

From her vantage point Tria, with her incredible vision and the illumination cast by daybreak, saw the hill of her pack and another opposite from which Jett had sung to her. Standing on a hill between them, with unknown territory to her north and to her south, she stood transfixed by her boundless options. Food did not cross her mind as her spirit was no less peaceful and enthusiastic as it was the night before when Joy spoke and The Last filled the air. Joy then pulled her tiny hard-shell body through Tria's fur and spoke from the tip of her paw.

"You are to be the famous one who vanquishes many to save all others. I will be at your side to help you survive, for much trouble is before you. It was your great sire and dam that taught you ways no other could. You must now use these lessons to fulfill your destiny." With that, Joy retreated into Tria's deep undercoat.

Personally, I always dreamed of Tria and her adventures, her strength, courage, intelligence, tenacity, and beauty. I like to think we terriers got many of our best qualities from her. Unfortunately, from her we've also inherited negative characteristics, like our impetuousness.

Nevertheless, Tria took Joy's ominous warning without fear or worry for in her life she only knew success, the previous day of rejection notwithstanding. Danger, pain, and failure were not within her comprehension. Gazing to the north and then to the south again, Tria fixed her stare to the north over the great distance visible from her vantage point, seeing the mountains curving to the west, narrowing the plain as it approached the sea. Then she trotted down from her nighttime shelter toward a vast valley.

Remember Tria was the strongest, fastest, and most dominant of the pups. Only her late-blooming littermate Jett might match her. And she was already well on her way to rivalling Versa's magnificence. So, this second generation of wolf perfection feared no creature. Being driven to the north, she moved quickly covering perhaps ten miles when the sun had finally occupied the downward side of the horizon. Her stride slowed as she smelled a fresh kill off to her side causing her to realize she had not yet eaten. As she changed direction, Joy struggled to the top of her host's hairy paw and began to glow. Joy blinked again and again. Tria took no notice.

Moving through a wood of heavy timber and thick underbrush she came upon a lynx with a marmot in its grasp. Weighing in at four-stone, Tria never had a run-in with a lynx and had no idea just how fast and strong that dynamo really was. Neither did she know that cat claws are much sharper weapons than those of wolves. She simply strode up to the feline expecting its retreat. But instead, quicker than any creature she had ever seen, it sprung itself into her face with claws and teeth aimed at her eyes and the top of her neck. Startled but unhurt, Tria flipped the attacker off the top of her head with a mighty shake. She backed away and the mini-monster cat just as quickly returned to its prey. Unharmed but undeterred, her mind tried to work the problem—wind and smell, no help. No good angle of attack, no element of surprise, and so on—including the inhibited bite and all the rest of her lessons—none offered utility to her. Almost immediately after her intellectual analysis of the situation failed, Tria felt a rage building until she became consumed with hate. The hate of the lone wolf bubbling inside her was amplified by the perfection of her genetics. Just then Joy emerged from her fur blinking and spoke to her. "You will not enjoy a marmot for it is not a meal suited for one as you, only for those not equal to your greatness." But ignoring Joy's influence she descended into an uncontrollable rage. The pain of her banishment still simmering beneath her consciousness and magnifying her anger, she refused to be dominated and defeated by another creature again. Then the uncontrollable explosion of her blind rage commenced and terminated in a bloody instant. The cat was now dead but Tria had a deep wound to her magnificent snout, and her right ear was torn, split part way up its height like kitchen shears had been applied. Blood poured from each wound as she left the dead lynx and the marmot where they lay.

It took some time for the blinding red fog of anger and heat of battle to subside from her consciousness. As dusk arrived almost unnoticed, Joy struggled through bloody fur and flew onto Tria's snout opposite the gash thereupon and said "You have NOT discerned well. Remember this lesson, the lesson of the lynx." And with that, Joy disappeared into the night sky to join The Last. Ignoring The Last, Tria wandered aimlessly for some distance before she began to think clearly again. Eventually she realized there would be much food in the great valley. Soon spying a hare with her predator's eyesight, she burst into a sprint and quickly had a meal. She repeated her culling of the Leporidae through the night until very little remained of the hare population in the valley.

13

With the sound of her brother Jett calling to her and the bleeding stanched by time and gluttony, Tria's head cleared enough to focus on the wolf song. She listened as Jett explained how Ellip discovered an emaciated young female scavenging on a meager carcass left over from the evening before. He explained the strange bargain offered by the little wolf while they confronted her trying to steal their paltry remnants.

Jett tried his best to explain in great detail the strange event. His song continued: "Ellip had pinned her to the ground with the inhibited bite, but I pushed her aside and stood over the little bitch determined to quickly implement her execution."

Again, Jett precisely quoted the intruder and told Tria what happened next. "As she cowered below me the little wolf quickly offered me a bargain." 'Much I know that threatens you,' she said. 'I have seen your ways and success which threaten many. I am but a starving annoyance to you posing no peril. Thus, should you kill me now you will have accomplished little. But then you will have lost the opportunity for me to provide you with the information you need to survive.' Jett continued to recount to Tria, "As I stood over her, confused by her words and her courage to speak to me with such bravado, Ellip told me to let her live long enough for her to speak."

Stopping for a few moments to gather his thoughts, Jett amplified his song to Tria explaining, "Ellip then said to the little wolf, should your information be valuable to us the carcass shall be yours, but should you be disingenuous we shall smell your lies and your destruction shall not be delayed."

Jett's song to Tria continued with a message of danger from the enemy wolf, and now Tria could hear the panic and helplessness in Jett's voice. "The little wolf said that Arn and Versa are expanding their territory and displacing more lone wolves. The lone wolves led by Ket the Elder were gathering to establish a truce with others to eliminate Arn, Versa, their five remaining adult offspring, and Bord. They schemed to attack Arn by outnumbering him while the rest of the pack was hunting and while Versa was in the den, for the smell of her pregnancy was obvious throughout the valley. Then they would finish off the rest. Without the leadership of the great alpha wolf Arn, surely the five adults and Bord would be unable to repel a surprise attack by a group of lone wolves two or three times their number." Then the song stopped. Such was the valuable information gained by Ellip's wise insistence on a stay of execution and precisely conveyed to Tria.

A new voice was heard coming from elsewhere, not the camp of Jett or Arn. It was Bord. He now understood Jett for the first time and could speak as well. Though Tria easily interpreted Jett's and Bord's musical stories, she had not yet learned how to offer her own long-distance communication. She could hear the fear in Bord's trembling voice as he repeated again and again that the smell of many lone wolves was surrounding the pack.

Tria wrestled with the great conflict between loyalty to her original pack and the hate she felt for being so treated, for being so poorly understood. She recalled her embarrassment in front of her now grown littermates at her banishment. Certainly, all the pups in Versa's new litter would someday soon also know of her failure. Filled with resentment she tried to ignore the airborne messages. Now independent, well-fed, and on her own, why should she care about those that abandoned her? Soulful songs from Jett in return told Bord that he could not abandon his camp to help them. But surely no number of lone wolves could take Arn's hill with The Magnificent Ones and Tria at their side. The last call of that evening was Bord desperately informing Jett that Tria had been banished.

Hearing all this from her lonely place, Tria noticed The Last in the distance and wondered why Joy was not there with her. But Joy's words last spoken to her about discernment now wrestled within Tria, fighting her lesser virtues including self-pity, an extremely rare emotion for a wolf. She could not imagine herself returning to aid those who so unjustly rejected her. Surely, she thought, her good intentions and superior knowledge were the real reasons for banishment. She concluded she was simply too good to be accepted. Tria sought comfort under a misshapen, twisted laurel bush attempting sleep, but it was restless, filled with dreams of killing Jett. Dream after dream she found herself dispatching her dear brother. As a helpless observer of her own dreamscape, her tortured mind kept trying to stop herself from such an evil deed, but she could only watch helplessly until on the final turn of the insane carousel of fratricide, he looked into her eyes and cried out for mercy.

Tria thrashed about in her sleep as if fighting a battle she could not win. Soon in her nightmares she saw a wolf battlefield and upon it Versa and all the others lying dead, with Arn standing upon them covered with their blood. In her dream she tried to move but could not. She could not run, or move, or fight. She could only helplessly struggle in terror as if bound by some mysterious force.

Later, in the waning hours of night, a strange and unintelligible wolf song was heard while she dozed in that near-awake, near-dream fog of the most objectionable and restless type of sleep. Was it real or imagined? When she might not have been able to take any more, the sound stopped her dreaming.

Her now semi-lucid mind only contained blackness and dread as she stared through the twisted branches into a bleak night sky that made her shudder. Unable to force her eyes shut again, fearing more dreams she stared upward through meaningless twists and curves of the laurel.

Now terrified by her seclusion, she could detect no smells, no sounds, no movement—nothing of any consequence any-where. The emptiness of night fell upon her like a wet blanket of complete and utter isolation, and she trembled. There was nothing perceptible to her great senses, except the barely visible twists of the laurel, dark charcoal bark upon a black night sky. Tria wondered to herself if she was dead.

Eventually tearing her thoughts away from her night terrors, she noticed herself breathing. Now certain she was alive and not dead she lay in a pool of dread forgetting just who she was. What was that song? Was it a dream or real? Then her mind returned to her affliction – abuse and unjust banishment. But after the night of terror, these feelings of self-pity were no longer satisfying but instead suddenly repulsive to her.

Tria got up not knowing how to stop the growing insanity and then threw herself into a patch of briars and needled thistles.

13

Lying in stickers and thorns that pulled at her fur and stung her skin, all her selfish and self-righteous thoughts of the evening now seemed inherently and utterly wrong. Tria flushed with panic. Her selfish thoughts were now replaced with a longing for Jett and her pack. She arose, stifled the wounds of her heart, and headed to the hill of her childhood.

Perhaps with greater speed than Versa had ever achieved, Tria ran until her nose told her to stop. She was downwind from five lone wolves who did not know of her presence. Understanding how to outflank a herd of herbivores, she took to the far side of the five assassins and without being detected, bulldozed the first interloper into the ground and ripped through its neck with such speed and ferocity that barely a sound was made. Her blood up, she prepared to attack the second enemy when she heard a familiar growl. It was Fic confronting the remaining four attackers. For some reason only he was there to defend their wolf camp. Fic stood there as one against four, fearlessly willing to give his life to help if necessary to help save the pack.

At once they converged on Fic as Tria fell upon them, first dispatching the one ripping into Fic's hindquarters and then the one on the top of his neck. Fic had another lone wolf on the ground and had eliminated its threat, but at a great cost. Tria leaped in front of the remaining enemy wolf as it was about to attack Fic. Its termination was swift and Tria again was not hurt. She licked Fic's wounds and after a moment she sped off.

Fic limped up the hill toward their sanctuary perplexed at what just happened. How did Tria eliminate four enemies in the time it took him to battle one? How was it she was not hurt? How was it she appeared almost out of nowhere and just as quickly disappeared? He realized he felt little pain while his courage and toughness remained steadfast.

Tria, still full of fight, was on the move. She wondered where the great Arn was when all this occurred. Soon Tria discovered why the great Arn was not there to dispatch the band of five would-be killers. As Fic came up far behind her at his own pace too slowly to be of help, Tria smelled many unknown wolves with their blood lust boiling over at the top of Arn's hill.

As fast as she could run, she arrived just in time to see the great Arn surrounded by six lone wolves, all about to attack. They rushed toward Arn guarding his precious den. He grabbed the first and shook it hard, breaking its neck, but by that time the others were upon him. Tria sprinting with a velocity never before achieved, split the group like a stand of bowling pins, knocking three off their feet. Arn quickly dispatched the one biting at his left side while Tria pulled off the one on the top of his neck with a rag doll shake, breaking its neck. As the fight concluded, four enemy attackers were overwhelmed by Tria, two by Arn. Minor injuries were received by the victors but none that would overtake Tria or Arn. In those brief moments of death, Versa was whelping her new litter.

14

Word of the failed *coup d'état* spread to all the surrounding river valleys and hills. Eleven lone wolves had been dispatched by Fic, Arn, and Tria. The legend of The First Wolf Pack grew across the land, but would the lone wolves come with more next time? And where was Bord? Why did he warn of the pending attack without remaining to defend the pack? Was this adopted uncle a coward or a traitor? She had always suspected Bord, the son of Ket the Elder.

Tria's mind spun out of control. Where were the other four besides Fic, Jett, and herself? As the night fell upon the resting battered victors, Arn called to Tria lying nearby, saying "Tonight we shall have a special Wolf Council." What did this mean, she wondered? Only weeks ago she had found herself banished for suggesting Council, yet now they saw fit to invite her?

As Arn lay his great, but slightly battered body down in front of the entrance to the den, Versa peered from inside the entrance, still reeking of giving birth. He directed Tria to take a place opposite of the den's entrance.

He looked to Fic and said, "Well done my loyal son. You have paid a heavy price for your pack. You, too, may stay for this special Council meeting."

With that, The Wolf Utterance—a sound only a wolf can understand, as it has no translation in your language—signaled the Council's opening. Hearing The Wolf Utterance Tria and Fic understood that until this moment they hadn't earned the privilege of belonging at the Wolf Council. The call to Council stirred in them an intense wolf emotion they had never felt before. It summoned up intense loyalty while making each of them feel insignificant without the pack.

First, Arn informed Tria why Bord and the others were not there. His nighttime communication must have occurred en route. They had been sent to join Jett to defend against a second, much larger group of lone wolves. Arn had instructed the team to first offer the lone wolves a choice between peace or annihilation.

Arn explained the alphas faced a life and death dilemma. "With a larger group of wolves assembling near Jett and Ellip, Versa and I realized the lone wolves' plan was to start with a battle against only two wolves, Jett and Ellip of the second wolf pack. We could not be sure of the number of those threatening us but we were certain that Jett and Ellip were in greater danger than we."

That was why Arn and Versa sent all the adult wolves to assist and protect Jett, Ellip, and their pups. Believing it to be a long shot, they hoped themselves to remain silent and still deep within the den, and thereby give the impression from a distance that their wolf camp was abandoned. Hopefully the lone wolves would see the large pack traveling to Jett's camp and assume none stayed behind, never coming near to investigate.

Bord, being the oldest, was to lead the other five of the pack to show overwhelming force and hopefully to deceive the attackers that all had departed from Arn's camp for Jett's hill. Upon arrival, surely no lone wolf would attack seven of the largest and strongest wolves ever known, those who possessed hunting and killing skills beyond imagination. They knew they could count on Ellip to join their forces as the eighth, if needed.

Arn continued to explain everything to Tria. "Only Fic somehow knew to return while Versa was about to deliver her second litter. He warned me to prepare, as many lurked about us ready to attack. He tracked the nearest group and intercepted them. He was willing to fight them as far away from the den as he could accomplish. That's when you came upon them." He then looked again at Fic and said "You know things before others. For this gift of yours Versa and I are extremely grateful."

Tria now understood everything about the threats of the lone wolves and the decision to send the others to Jett. Arn continued to speak as the alpha, the leader who would not be challenged. He then spoke of cooperation, tolerance, loyalty, self-control, and discernment, these most-powerful wolf virtues. Words didn't come easily to Arn, who mostly communicated through his actions, but that day Fic and Tria found themselves amazed at his clear expressions of wisdom.

As he paused, Tria asked permission to speak. Arn was delighted and granted her a right to speak at Council. He knew only Tria could articulate these wolf virtues in a way they all could understand, as she had done for Jett. Arn's self-awareness was pure and complete. He knew he was a wolf of action, not words.

Tria cautiously presented her thoughts. "Should we survive and be a pack again, I beg permission from the alphas to explain to the others all the lessons of The Wolf Ways as I have compiled them."

Arn and Versa were delighted, for they knew only she could articulate this information clearly and precisely. Arn replied, "Yes Tria, you are right in all you said. My daughter, it is these lessons that allowed us to be one, to be successful and safe." Then he looked at Versa, who gave him a confirming nod that he had spoken wolf-truth.

Tria felt overwhelmed with the honor of Arn and Versa's acceptance of her request to speak and the chance that someday she might share her knowledge with others. It was the first time Tria dared call them The Wolf Ways. Arn, Versa, and Fic all nodded in appreciation as Tria coined the phrase that would continue for innumerable centuries.

All waited with anticipation for Arn—still holding his head high in complete stillness—to speak again. The greatest of wolves addressed new, heretofore unknown things to his two offspring. He spoke of how he and Versa had fought and almost died, how Versa saved his life, and how they committed to the creed, "If one is to live, we both must live." Their two offspring sat mute, overwhelmed by the thought of such a battle.

Suddenly the clear voice of Jett, then joined by Bord, revealed their circumstances. Believing no attack was imminent, the other four were returning to The First Wolf Pack after all had failed in their mission to broker peace. Jett lamented after the others left, "There are gathering in the far-off distance more lone wolves than we can count."

Perhaps instinctively, Bord decided to stay behind with Jett and Ellip just in case he would be needed.

Arn then looked to his cherished partner Versa and said, "The Wolf Ways will not fail me, for I must not fail you." With that Arn made The Wolf Utterance signaling the Council's adjournment.

15

Tria found a place to lie not too close to the den where she contemplated all that had occurred. Had she really dispatched eight wolves herself and suffered nary a scratch? Did she really run faster than any wolf had ever run? Did she really hear The Wolf Utterance of the Council? Was she really allowed to speak at the Council? Did she really understand what Jett and Bord had said?

As she put her head upon her paws, Joy climbed out of her fur and flew onto her cheek fur whispering, "You are the princess who must vanquish many to save many more."

With that Joy disappeared as Arn approached with a meal of fresh mutton he had just slain to nourish his hero-daughter and the others. She wondered what kind of ultra-magnificent wolf he was. She also wondered why he wasn't doing something to help Jett and Ellip. She did not know exactly what, but something had to be done.

Tria's great nose confirmed that no lone wolf danger was near, so she ate and slept. But her dreams brought only nightmares. Countless wolves surrounded her cherished Jett, and his dear Ellip, and their young litter. The wolves kept coming from every direction, snarling, and foaming at the mouth. Bord was covered by a dozen lone wolves as he fought to no avail. She awoke and wondered if wolf dreams could tell the future. Then she heard a sweet gentle buzz and saw Joy again. Joy blinked a few times and said to her, "You must not avoid your destiny." Tria felt a strong determination building, but it was devoid of any peace. In confusion and panic she began to plan.

How many lone wolves would have to die for Arn's and Jett's packs to survive? Could she kill enough to stop them? Was it time to change from defense to offense? Perhaps she might find a preferable alternative? Why did Bord seek life outside the ways of the lone wolf? Wouldn't those who saw the success of the pack wish, like Bord, to emulate them? If only she could make them understand. But she could not get past the danger posed to Jett, and thus her blood began to boil with hatred and rage at what was happening. She grew obsessed with killing as many as it took to rid all lone wolves from upon the land, from the endless string of mountains on the east to the shore of the ocean to the west. She regurgitated her meal of mutton and did not re-eat. She was now one of them. The poisoned blood only one generation removed would not be denied.

Crossing in front of Arn stationed at the entrance of the den she walked off without a glance or a nod. Arn made no sound as he watched her depart. Tria knew what she had to do. Arn could sense the rage and hate boiling within his daughter but chose not to move from his defensive position of his den. Fic was at Arn's side when the Magnificent One placed himself against his son's punctured flesh to hasten healing, just as Versa had done for him. Fortunately, Fic's wounds made by sharp canine teeth did not tear but only punctured, making the healing, once cleaned, much quicker than Arn's ordeal.

The path to the north and the path to Jett were both well known to Tria. She did not choose north. Arriving with the smell of many lone wolves near, but not close enough to Jett's pack for her to sneak past them, she tested the wind. She counted the individual smells. Surely, she could fight off twelve?

16

Remember, my friends, that Tria was just over two years old. Most of us large wolves aren't fully developed until we are three, but she was always ahead of the rest. Now this package of wolf perfection reflected the young image of her mother, Versa, with the added genetics of the powerful Arn. At least such is what she thought to herself when she detected the hot breath of a large male wolf on her neck; she forgot the wind. Just a bit quicker and stronger than her surprise attacker she spun around and took him to the ground in one movement, like nothing the enemy wolf had ever seen. But for some reason she inhibited her bite, holding him to the ground with her overwhelming power, not completing her self-defense. She found herself amazed at her adversary's power as she struggled to hold him. It was then the other eleven lone wolves arrived. Only a few hours before the new day's dawning, and seemingly out of nowhere, thousands of fireflies filled the air between them. The intensity of their light was like nothing Tria had previously seen. The Last caused the entire group to stand perplexed, nearly blinding them in a cloud of blinking lights. At this, Joy emerged from Tria's fur, flew to her battered ear, and whispered, "Ask him his name."

Tria released just enough pressure on her adversary's neck for him to speak and then did as Joy directed.

He said, "I am Ket the Elder."

Tria inquired, "Why do you want to kill me?"

"We are starving and we are being forced to poorer lands," he replied. "Your prosperity has caused great hatred and death among my kind. Why do you persecute us?"

Now Tria had only known one lone wolf before all the recent confrontations and that was Bord who was the omega dog in their pack. She wondered who the victim was and who the perpetrator was in this impossible scene.

"Ket," she said, "I have been north and there is much food there. Will you not travel until you have all you need?"

"Surely," he said, "mountains too great to scale are to the far north. And all the wolves to the south will object."

Tria responded, "Today I have killed eight lone wolves with nary a scratch, and I am prepared to kill you and all of your cohorts."

Tria continued, "I know who you are. You are Ket the Elder, the evilest of lone wolves. You steal and kill beyond that of all others with your deceptions." As she struggled mightily to hold him down, she continued. "It is you I am certain who has gathered this rabble to fight us. But we will not be vanquished, no matter how many you enlist. Will you discuss a way we may all prosper or shall I kill you now? Your choice."

Suddenly the glow of The Last dissipated, as Ket screamed, "We only know killing."

With that she took on the twelve. Jett and Bord arrived just in time for her defense, or surely she would have been overtaken. Somehow as the fight erupted, Ket the Elder used the commotion to escape.

A battle ensued like no other, three wolves of The First Wolf Pack against eleven lone wolves within a place thick with massive trees, towering to sky with trunks so immense a wolf could hide behind one and not be seen. Whether attacking or retreating, no animal could be sure how to avoid unintentionally ramming itself into these immovable giants.

Bord acting first, attacked the two lone wolves nearest him. Standing side by side between a pair of trees, two sets of deadly fangs attempted defense of Bord's frontal assault. Knowing his foes could not quickly turn around, caught between the colossal trunks, Bord attacked. Skillfully, in a perfect outflanking maneuver he dove under and between the two with an explosive lunge sufficient to instantly place himself behind them. After his clever tactic through his enemies' legs, Bord had them from behind as they were unable to defend themselves. They had unwittingly placed themselves in a trap.

Jett had grown beyond what she had remembered, and he now matched Arn in size and strength. He took on the two wolves in front of him just as another leaped from behind its screen of peeling bark. But they were no match for this mature and powerful wolf. Effortlessly he dispatched one on his left side as he tossed the other into the air and then terminated the third as it tried to take out his forelegs.

Tria did as she had done before without distraction by what was occurring around her. She somehow avoided the jaws of four wolves simultaneously confronting her. With her incredible speed and fury, she piled up her enemies one upon another, upon the next. Jumping left, right, and above them, none could lay their fangs upon her. She turned from her fourth victim and saw one approaching Jett from behind. As it attempted to land upon Jett's back to take his neck within the lone wolf's jaws, Tria burst from where she stood in an impossible broad jump and intercepted the villain in mid-air. Knocking it to the ground she tore through its neck in one almost effortless move. As her comrades turned to see if all enemies lay vanquished, they saw Tria accelerate after the last of the eleven adversaries as it retreated. Tria's final fight, hidden from Bord's and Jett's view, took place behind the ultimate wooden giant which towered in the center of the battlefield. It ended quickly as they heard the sound of death snap through the air like the crack of a whip. Somehow, even among the obstacles, the battle was over in only a few brief moments.

Jett had thought surely now the word of their superior strength and tenacity would fill the land and forestall more canine killing. He believed that in the face of the superiority of the wolf pack even Ket the Elder would not wish to fight, no matter how great an evil plot he could contrive. But he was more than wrong in his hopefulness.

Perhaps it was Jett's easygoing, confident nature that predisposed him to optimism. Certainly, it made him a skillful leader, but it did not prevent that day's battle; Tria killed six, five were dispatched by the others, including three by Jett.

As the now possessed Tria stood upon the corpses, she screamed, "Ket the Elder has escaped!" and with that she began to foam at the mouth while the blood of many wolves dripped from her face, legs, and body.

Bord observed Tria's bloodlust surpassed both Jett's and his, now fearing she enjoyed the killing. Her eyes enlarged with the chilling intensity of an uncontrollable obsession. The conflict over, Jett called to the others to follow him back to his camp. Arriving, they found Jett's den empty and Ellip and the pups missing.

Tria was temporarily shaken out of her bloodlust. Was it Jett's arrival to help her the reason for the disappearance of Ellip and the pups? Was she herself responsible? Did other lone wolves destroy Jett's family? Again, Tria's head spun out of control.

Jett stood motionless at the entrance to the first den he had dug until he collapsed. Bord and Tria sniffed him, then lay against him. Tria remembered her shedding of the rarest of things, a wolf-tear. She saw such grief in Jett's countenance but no tear fell. After only a moment he stood up, thanked them for their pack support, and then said, "My nose will surely find my beloved Ellip and my young."

They all three put their noses to the wind and to the ground, looking for a trail, or a scent-laden breeze. Even though drenched in the ghastly goo of killing, and in spite of a hot and powerful wind scraping the dry soil like a shovel, Tria was the one who soon picked up the scent and called to the others, "I have found her trail. Follow me."

Now we know that Ellip was lovely beyond description, perhaps the most beautiful she-wolf to ever live, but remember she was also very shrewd. She had quickly snatched her litter, each by the scruff and carried them off to a cave she had long ago discovered, with many fallen trees upon it. It was the hibernation home of a great bear. Now this giant of the valley, foothills, and the forest was far from his craggy den, gorging himself on berries. So Ellip placed her precious brood into a fissure inside the cave, near the entrance. She took a position upon a high place that allowed her to see both the bear and her abandoned camp in the distance. The camp was too far away and the line of sight too interrupted with trees for her to see her allies making their way toward her. From there, Ellip thought she could launch any necessary attack. She only hoped that circumstances did not require her to be in two places at the same time.

As feared, the great bear lumbered toward its soon-to-be-winter home, and Ellip knew she might only temporarily fight him off. But while clashing with the great bear, what would become of her little ones? Cleverer than any fox, she ran into the tallest grasses under a stand of trees, flushing a deer in front of the bear and into the field before him. There the giant saw her take down the deer and begin dragging it in his direction. Ellip knew he could not resist fresh meat. As he charged her, she put up mock resistance and then retreated to the side of the field touching the woods that provided a hidden path to the cave and the rescue of her young.

Ellip gathered her pups and began to make her way back to the den. Jett, Tria, and Bord, now moving away from the den and in her direction, soon spotted her. Overcome with happiness and relief they greeted her with wagging tails and licking tongues.

Jett called out "My beloved! My little ones! Come to me that I may never be separated from you all again."

And with this Ellip slammed against his side with a loving and glancing blow. "My Jett, we are all fine. None of our precious little ones were harmed."

Once the excited greeting slowed down, Ellip explained: "I heard and smelled a second group of lone wolves gathering on the opposite side of the hill from where you three confronted the others. I had no time to waste, so I took the pups and fled."

As they returned to the camp, Tria realized she and the others did not even know that another group of lone wolves had gathered. Perhaps it was only by her picking up Ellip's scent that they vacated Jett's camp in time or they might have fallen into a trap. But now upon their return to the camp with the pups, the smell of lone wolves was waning. The search for Ellip had been enough of a delay for Ket the Elder to call the second group to retreat after the slaughter of his cohorts at the jaws of Tria, Jett, and Bord. Now safe, Ellip placed the pups back in their den, descending deeply into it to nurse them.

Tria had somehow vanquished fourteen lone wolves and their blood stained her muzzle, neck, and forepaws. It made her appear in the approaching moonlight as a red demon, with cold blue eyes that pierced the now crimson fur like those of automobile headlights in the fog. Her lynx-damaged ear gave her a look of a three-horned monster. Jett looked at his beloved sister and thanked her for her protection; she did not respond. As the last bit of undried blood dropped from her cheek fur, she focused only on the next battle. With Tria now in the pack, Ellip feared for her progeny.

When the pups were nursed and the warriors rested, Tria was consumed with the idea that Bord might have betrayed The First Wolf Pack. How else was it that Ket the Elder was able to escape? While Bord and Jett had just fought by her side, her paranoia remained inescapable. Tria imagined that he might even kill his own allies to maintain his clever deception. "Why didn't Arn prevent this one from betraying us?" she mumbled.

Jett, straining, did not understand what was said and simply ignored it, as his focus stayed on his pack.

Tria and the others tried to rest for recovery from trauma can't be avoided indefinitely, only postponed. But while needing respite, Tria feared sleep for her dreams of the night before terrified her so. She found a place away from the others on Jett's hill and stared into the night sky as the others slept.

17

All wolves (the wild ones) and we dogs (the new-wolves) grieve the part of our history when we first denied, then fought The Wolf Ways. The poisoned blood that was part of the foundation of our strength to survive was also the lone wolf's demise. It clouded our perception of threats and created almost human-type paranoia. And like your race, a super-response trigger could be tripped that blinded the agitated one to all reason including the inhibited bite. And I regret to say, for your race, too, there is much avoidable bloodshed in your history.

Jett knew his sister better than anyone, and he did not fear her, but he also trusted Ellip and her instinct to detect threats and to protect her pups. He knew the only ones who could make everything right were Arn and Versa. And if they could not reach Tria, they and only they could vanquish her. For as equally matched as Jett might be with his sister, he knew she had an instinct to kill so intense and so contrary to his easy-going confidence that he might not stand a chance against her if her blood was up.

Jett's heart ached as he struggled to understand what gave his sister, the most gifted of wolves, such a split personality. There was his Tria with whom he bonded and played, sharing their every thought with great trust and respect and for whom he had a special closing verse to his nighttime songs. Then there was the one who almost reveled in the bloodshed as she raged with violence and with such intensity to scare his beloved Ellip. He always struggled to understand how one so near to physical perfection and with boundless intelligence could have gotten herself banished, unless she was deeply flawed. While this assessment haunted him, his love for his sister prevented him from fully accepting it.

His mind began to analyze all that was happening. If Arn was so wise as to send Bord to join him to pursue a brokered peace, albeit with reinforcements, he must also have a contingency plan. He called out that night with the greatest wolf song possibly ever sung. Jett's voice resounded with the story of how Tria helped him and Bord and of Ellip's clever retreat. He sang of his great sister's tenacity in battle, singularly taking on and defeating six lone wolves. So great was Jett's refrain, and now so bonded into a pack of single-minded purpose, all those at the first wolf camp completely understood him.

All in Jett's camp listened, shocked, when a rich baritone punctured the night sky in reply.

The Great Arn's voice rang out, "Thank you, my son, for the gift of long-distance communication. All of you must now listen and heed my words. We must be one pack again."

Tria burst from her restless faux sleep, leaping into the air like her legs were spring-loaded. As she, Jett, Ellip, and Bord listened intently, Ket's spies lurked about the hills, trying to keep watch on these most-powerful ones. When Tria jumped up, one lone wolf spy saw the crimson glow of her blood-laden fur and the heights attained in her near magical levitation, concluding that she was no mere wolf, but something of another type of mysterious creation. Now the legend of Tria the ghostly she-wolf spread farther and faster than ever.

When Arn's voice fell silent, Ellip and Jett gathered their pups. Bord, too, carried some in his now gentle jaws. Tria led the way while the rest tried to keep up with her pace. She carried none of Ellip's pups.

18

The First Wolf Pack was reunited as the eastern sky began to glow with early morning anticipation. All the wolves of The First Wolf Pack, along with newcomers Bord and El-lip, swarmed around the den, almost hysterical with glee. Even the stoic Arn wagged his tail frantically as he carefully smelled each pack member to verify their identity, determine each wolf's condition, and temper his worry. Versa more calmly greeted each of them as their reunification temporarily washed away the recent dangers past and those anticipated.

But their grateful gathering could not long distract any of them from the foul smell at the foot of the hill they called home; lone wolf carcasses of the battle there began to rot. The bearded bone crushers of the sky eagerly awaited their chance to feed as they circled overhead in ever-increasing numbers while the other scavengers did the preliminary work. Typically wolves revile any scavenger, but to The First

Wolf Pack their presence was insignificant, notwithstanding the stench.

The now-combined packs had been through too much and had more yet to do for even their sensitive snouts to rule the moment. Versa stood next to Arn, with six now fully-mature wolves flanking them creating a fearsome halo of safety. Versa's second, smaller litter of five remained hidden in the den. Jett and Ellip entered this domain slowly, they and Bord dropping Ellip's pups near the center, as everyone watched the clumsy antics of thirteen week old pups Tria stood a few feet back, locked in a stare with Arn. Perhaps it was her time of puppy obedience, her insecurity of still not having her own pack, or the insanity of her dreams, but she looked away first, submitting to the great male wolf who called the original pack back together.

Arn ordered the five adults who remained living in his pack, with Bord temporarily replacing the injured Fic, to hunt for the group as directed. Versa had begun to call those of her first litter that remained with The First Wolf Pack, "the loyal five." The three adult visitors were to remain with him, Versa, and Fic. Tria spoke up, suggesting to Arn that she or Jett take Bord's place. Her distrust of Bord still seethed within her. Disregarding his daughter's suggestion, Arn instructed the hunters to form a wedge with the wind at their backs instead of in their faces—no lone wolves would surprise them. The mighty alpha ordered the modified loyal five to use their eyes to hunt and their ears and noses for defense. Moving with almost one mind, they sped through woods and thicket to eventually take a grazing beast without much effort, dragging it back to the hilltop where all others awaited. They set out again and quickly returned with more sustenance. Arn and Versa ate first, Jett came forward next simultaneously with Tria to whom he easily and instantly deferred. Then while the others ate, Arn sprinted to the highest part of their province. He observed six other hills with valleys and streams meandering therein. Returning to his expanded pack he surprised them all by making The Wolf Utterance without warning. A surprise expanded Wolf Council was called.

At the crushing sound of the call to Council, Versa's five puppies trembled in their den while the six cousins frantically sought shelter there. For wolves, all relations born of different brood bitches in the same season are considered cousins.

Versa laid her great physique across its opening while all the other wolves settled down immediately on the spot where they stood, regardless of comfort. With Council called to order, all obediently dropped in their places; though Tria, last as usual, took her time getting settled in her place.

Arn fixed his gaze upon each of them, one at a time, pausing briefly to await submission. Coming to Tria last he moved toward her, not breaking his stare while ever so slightly showing his teeth. Seemingly towering above her she did not return the stare but looked away.

As they listened in rapt attention, the alpha male explained: "Bord's only surviving littermate, Casso has spoken with me as she fought the vultures to scavenge on the rotting carcasses at the base of our hill. She begged I not kill her and pleaded that she might be spared from starvation. She explained most lone wolves felt driven to fight for survival because of The First Wolf Pack and now Jett's pack too."

Arn's voice boomed like thunder as he said, "My daughter, you have sealed the fate of many with your blood lust. The inhabitants of the entire land of these hills and all lands beyond now talk of an evil and ghostly she-wolf that must be eliminated. They have not been intimidated; they have become enraged."

He continued to address the group, "When Tria spoke with Ket, she might have killed the leader of their enemies but let him slip away, and then again when Tria led Jett and Bord in the killing of his would-be allies. She very well might have missed the chance to broker peace had she killed Ket and then reasoned with the others." Arn then ended The Wolf Council, and all shunned Tria.

Our super-warrior wolf Tria panicked. How could she be blamed for disposing of fourteen of their enemies? Only a short time ago she and Fic were honored, temporary Council members. She felt confused. Would her good intentions be misunderstood a second time? What did Ket the Elder have planned next? Who was this Casso—Bord's collaborator? Her mind racing out of control, Tria contemplated killing Arn and taking control over The First Wolf Pack. But the power of The Wolf Utterance used to call the Council incapacitated her bloodlust just long enough to slow the furious boil of her ill intent down to a simmer. Fortunately for us all, she managed to restrain herself, for even the great Arn might have been unable to beat her.

My friends, you will certainly never experience a Wolf Council, so I will try to help you understand. When The Wolf Utterance is made, no adult pack wolf can ignore it or disobey it. It is the profound call to be what you were created to be, a member of the pack without bias or ego. Think about the most compelling thing you have ever read, or the most moving scene from a play or movie that has aroused in you a spirit of determination and intense inspiration like no other. Well, that feeling you have experienced is but a fraction of what is conveyed by the alpha when The Wolf Utterance is made.

Council may be brief, or it may be protracted, but it only deals with what must be shared and no more. Nothing else would ever be allowed by the alpha pair. There is no chit chat or gossip. This includes the commitment of each to the survival of the pack and much more only a wolf's soul can fully comprehend. It stirs the very lifeblood and genetic memory of each wolf like nothing else for any other beast in all of creation.

Fortunately, after so much death and destruction a temporary peace lay upon the land. The loyal five with Bord still replacing Fic, hunted again after patrolling a vast radius around their hill to ensure the safety of the rest. As the ostracized Tria walked away from her childhood home, she went alone to that nearby place where she had cried. She lay upon the barren earth trying to feel something other than abandonment and rejection, but it only reinforced her despair. It was lucky for all that this rock of desolation also chilled her avenging heart.

19

Arn's extended family enjoyed the meals delivered by the hunting team, and the puppies slowly overcame the trauma of hearing Arn's Council call. Even Ellip's pups at thirteen weeks are vulnerable to a fear response.

Prime health was being restored to Fic of the loyal five. He had only one moderately-serious puncture wound to his hindquarter from helping Arn and Tria fight off lone wolf invaders. Remember that Tria had licked his wound to clean and soothe it, and this touched Fic. How could such a vicious beast show him compassion, he wondered?

After that day's meal Fic observed the still shunned Tria venturing off alone again. He realized that with the wind in her face, he could probably follow cautiously without detection. Fic could not help but feel concern and love for his great, but flawed sister. Somehow in his mind he knew she was in much turmoil. He perceived more than viciousness in her wide-eyed stare after the last battle. Staying far back, he remembered how she had dominated him when they were younger, and he shuddered to think how many lone wolves she had killed by herself. He certainly never wanted to get on her bad side.

Fic watched as Tria carefully examined a barren rock, circling and sniffing for a very long time, then watched her seemingly collapse onto the empty and hard place as if all life had been sucked out of her. Seeing this odd behavior, he recalled the first Wolf Way and how Tria had perhaps saved both him and Arn, successfully fighting alongside Jett and Bord. This incident most justifiably aroused Fic's wolf loyalty. With a crouch and his tail dropped in submission, he carefully approached her, moving slowly until absolutely certain she could see and hear him, for a surprise would prove most unwise. With dusk approaching, wolf senses heighten. This is the worst time to startle a wolf.

Recognizing Tria was well aware of his approach, he crawled on his belly the last few feet until his muzzle was next to his littermate. He pressed gently against her muzzle and then rolled on his back, mimicking play. He repeated this until Tria stood. Fic spoke first, "My great sister, let us leave this place together soon for I sense it makes you unhappy."

She bowed with her forepaws a bit then slid the side of her body against his and wagged her great tail. She again, albeit ever so slightly, felt like part of the pack. Fic looked deeply into Tria's eyes and grew confused. He wondered what he just saw in the eyes of his regal sister. He felt concern for her as the clarity of his vision identified a near insanity of emptiness bound up with hate and confusion.

As they loped back to join the rest, Fic noticed a small spot of light deep within her fur just above her left ear. This light made no sense to him and although he found it pleasant, said nothing of it. In an attempt to remind her of wonderful things in her past he called out, "Let's race! Let's see which one of us can get to the camp first." With that Fic took off running. Tria, giving him a head start, decided to play along. Accelerating, she passed him just feet from the boundary of the camp. She always willed to win.

The next day after the loyal five had fed the pack, Fic felt ready to rejoin them. But first he wanted to return to that lonely place to investigate. He snuck from the pack while Tria and the others ate. He paid special attention with his nose as he approached the spot. As he used his great snout to examine the place, it burned as if something acidic and cold was there. Investigating it further, he realized it was actually profound nothingness. He felt a terrifying level of despair and loneliness and a great need to be with Tria. Have you not had the experience of being ill and noticed how your dog wants to be close to you and provide comfort? Like Fic, we new-wolves do not like to see any of our pack unhappy or suffering.

With his head swirling in confusion Fic recalled the pack's joy in togetherness until the great ones banished Tria. But soon after her departure, they all regained their happiness. Now, although they allowed her back into the reunited pack, they ignored her. All this confused him as he pondered what it was he had just seen in her eyes.

Standing near Tria's rock, this cold and joyless place made him shudder and ponder life without a pack. As he lifted his paw to touch this empty place, he pulled it back in horror before making contact. This most-sensitive wolf could feel the loneliness jump through the air and into his heart like a lightning bolt mating tree to sky. This terrible feeling soon became insight to him into all the other wolves living a solitary existence. Fic realized it was this and more that he had seen in Tria's blue eyes.

He remembered what Arn had said about the lone wolf's possible desire for understanding. He suddenly had insight into Tria's misery. Without a pack the others must be very unhappy, and Fic wondered why only he and his pack led such an existence. On this historic day, this uniquely sensitive wolf, Fic, would be the first to feel empathy for a foe, not just tolerance. He had seen Arn and Versa exercise tolerance, but his was a deeper insight; he now understood its justification, not just for the weak and emaciated but for all who suffered, even those who hated him.

Fic's special empathy for his sister, however, was intensely heartfelt; he pondered how his physically-perfect sister could be so broken inside? He had seen Tria when her kill-switch was tripped, which wasn't necessarily a bad thing as most likely Tria had saved him and Arn in battle, but it was terrifying nonetheless. Had Arn and Versa only failed in their efforts to inculcate Tria, or were others also broken? And Fic wondered whether he might find out why Tria did not inhibit her bite or use wolf postures to intimidate others before attacking. He looked down at that barren, frigid rock but again did not touch it. At that moment as he realized the loneliness of this place, he wondered if he saw and felt something else. He contemplated whether ignorance and self-pity lurked there too. Then he looked to the darkening sky and sprinted home.

20

When Fic returned to the pack, the loyal five had provided much food and the brood bitches were regurgitating raw meat for the jumble of pups. All were having their fill of prime sustenance, although Tria ate in a place away from the others. Fic approached her again, but she only glanced at him briefly before returning to her meal.

He called out to her from a safe distance, "My sister Tria, I am your loyal brother. Oh, that I might lay closer to you."

Getting no response, he took pains to ensure she understood he posed no threat to her meal. As he drew near, stopping with a few feet separating them, he laid to Tria's side while looking off in a direction about ninety degrees away from her face. This way he would suggest to her, without aggressive posture, that he might get closer to her when she finished her dinner. All night Fic lay nearby. Eventually, with a series of small movements, he positioned himself closer, with his face aimed a bit more toward hers.

During the night Fic watched his sister's restless sleep as the demons in her dreams caused her body to convulse in little fits and starts; eventually he could watch no more. Moving against her, he pressed the weight of his back against her shoulders to reassure her; her nightmares seemed to end as an intense chill entered Fic's body. But he did not move. Although she was asleep, he knew she could feel the warmth and comfort of his touch. Fic deemed it necessary to absorb much loneliness into himself for the sake of Tria and his pack.

In the morning Fic awoke with frozen shards of sadness throughout his body, but he could deal with that. He knew they would dissipate. The night had been a success, and now he looked forward to the new day.

He took inventory of their camp and found all of The First Wolf Pack, including the second generation, present and accounted for, except for Arn. Fic looked to Versa for reassurance, approaching her sideways, his tail wagging slightly. She sniffed his muzzle, then his hindquarter and walked away, telling him nothing. Noticing Jett standing with his chest fully expanded and his eyes fixed to a dense stand of thicket partially obscured by a large boulder that stood sentry on the north side of Arn's hill, Fic knew something was afoot. He saw Tria, eyes unflinching as she stared at Bord. He wondered what filled her dreams and what it might mean.

Fic always was the most sensitive of wolves, reading much through a sixth sense that still remains in us today. Some of you think it is our special sense of smell that recognizes emotions. But while acute smell tells us much, it does not tell us everything we know.

Jett, the guest alpha male, pricked up his ears. The wind to his back as a strong gust stirred leaves and dirt alike, Jett could not distinguish what lay disguised in the thicket, but his instincts pulsed on red alert. As he contemplated investigation, he felt Versa's cold stare on his neck. Turning to confirm his discomfort, he saw her stare and knew he must remain with them all.

Versa instructed all the adult wolves to form a broad circle of a diameter that put each of them uncomfortably far apart. The pups and Ellip were to occupy the den. As they fell in line with Versa's direction, time stood still for what Fic thought was a bit too long, even for Arn. Suddenly bursting from the thicket, around the massive oval rock Arn appeared and made a straight line to the center of Versa's circle. He instructed all: "Remain vigilant, imminent danger has passed but other threats are lurking." He then summoned Tria: "My daughter, join Versa and me in the center of our circle." All the other wolves closed the circle slightly to compensate for Tria's absence. Now with all ears fixed on Arn and what he would say, the great wolf demanded they train all their senses on what lay beyond the circle. No eavesdropping would be permitted. Of course, each wolf complied.

As Tria came face-to-face with Arn he instructed her to lie down. He and Versa then settled down next to her in regal and powerful postures. They noticed her ripped ear and the gash now healing on her muzzle. Versa wondered if this was how a lone wolf looked as it began its decline—battered, fighting, and sadly alone. The mother wolf would not allow this to be the future of the one who had all the greatest of attributes.

They began to address Tria. No other wolf heard anything although all knew the reclining wolves were in dialogue. Tria now learned of the contingency plan that Jett correctly believed must exist. As the details of the strategy unfolded, Tria began to grow impatient for action.

With this Arn called out to all the others to report what, if anything, they heard, saw, or smelled. With no threats detected he called them together and the defensive circle collapsed into a comfortably-close cohort. He explained he met a young wolf named Casso in the thicket as several lone wolves lurked a short distance away. Apparently now, with the senses of the entire pack probing and finding nothing near, the lurking threat had retreated. He described that Casso was dangerously emaciated and fearful. He discerned that she posed no threat, and with this explanation he made one loud, brief guttural growl. Casso slinked out of the thicket and cowered as all the original wolf pack loomed over her with their teeth bared.

Before the alphas of The First Wolf Pack could take their expected lead, Ellip stepped forward and said, "It is you, the clever little one; your words were true."

With this Jett and Ellip, like house guests not quite fitting in after realizing they might have insulted their host, found nearby their own place of detachment and comfort from the group. Little Casso was next approached by Versa, who sniffed her carefully and turned away. Permission was granted by Versa, alpha bitch. All could stand down. Then Fic approached the stranger, stopping a yard from her personal space, sniffed the air, stared at her, his tail wagging ever so slightly and briefly, then turned away. All the other members of Arn's pack ignored Casso.

Fic observed that Tria might be about to launch herself upon the invited intruder, then suddenly she appeared temporarily distracted. Once again, he noticed the small light next to Tria's ear. Fic took this odd interruption to move between Casso and Tria. Opportunity taken, he stared into his dominant sister's eyes, a long deep stare, but it was not one of aggression. Tria did not take it as such. Instead, she recalled her companion of the previous night who helped change her nightmares into restful sleep, whose body had drawn ghastly visions from her slumbering mind.

As Tria moved toward poor Casso, Fic feared destruction and considered intervention. Tria, however, avoided his blocking position. Certainly, Tria would have stared him down or intimidated him out of the way, but to his amazement, Tria went around him and then showed the malnourished young wolf the way to the day's leftover meat. Fic followed closely. The skinny young one was terrified of the ghostly she-wolf of legend and trembled inside, but her hunger overcame the fear, and she ate more than she had ever eaten before. When finally sated, Tria showed her to a small and fast stream cutting between an outcropping of rocks on the opposite side of Arn's hill where Casso had met him. While the visitor enjoyed wonderfully-cool refreshment, Tria stood watch. Casso trembled inside once again. Fic kept near, looking at this odd pair, a strange duo of fear and domination, of weakness and power—and he would not depart from them. Now bloated like a terrier stealing and eating the family's holiday turkey, Casso waddled toward the group scattered about and resting.

She spied a bald, flat rock on her way back to the cohort and even at a distance it scared her, smelling of more loneliness than she had ever known even in her meager existence, so she gave it an unusually-wide berth. Casso flinched as Tria suddenly accelerated past her and led the way into the encampment, showing her a place of scattered evergreen leaflets and bows that would be free of fleas. Opposite this comfortable place Casso saw Ellip lying across the entrance to the den housing the double litter. Versa lay above her on the arch of rock and hard soil that formed a portico for the den doubling the guard. Casso marveled at how three grand she-wolves could peacefully occupy one wolf camp.

As the last songbirds of the evening ended their squabbles, but while ample light remained for the eyes of wolves, Arn stood without a noise looking at Tria, and she understood she must follow. The two of them walked toward the stream and the rock of desolation. Tria spoke first.

"I object vigorously to your plan. Bord and Casso are likely spies, collaborators, saboteurs! We must not trust them."

He looked into his daughter's eyes and gently said, "I can smell liars and what is even more, there is one in our pack who can look into their wolf-souls. Bord and Casso are with us. You shall say no more."

Reaching their desolate destination, Arn stopped directly at the rock and its chill conducted through him like a dive into an icy stream. Shocked, Tria blurted out, "How is it you do not crumble my father? Surely the rock devastates your wolf soul." With that he bellowed a wail that pierced the silence and Tria's soul, and he stepped off the rock.

Civil twilight had become astronomical twilight, which is the weakest of lights before darkness rules—a wolf's favorite time. He went to the side of his bloodstained daughter. Neither moved. A private, two-wolf Council would be called.

21

As Joy elevated out of Tria's fur, many more of The Last appeared. They began to shine their intermittent gentle light, and Arn felt the chill of the rock leave him. As this tiny light show continued Arn let out a uniquely gentle and quiet wolf utterance. Tria came to his side and the two enjoined in their Wolf Council. Arn expressed his gratitude to Tria for her now true understanding that tolerance was one of the fruits of the wolf pack. He did this because he knew it was not firmly set in her heart and wished to reinforce the good. He explained, "I saw in a wolf dream how Versa had saved me. In my ignorance I thought the injury I sustained was Versa's fault, but in my dream I saw the truth. It was then I cried a wolf-tear giving this rock its first chill. In my ignorance and self-pity, I blamed the one who had saved me. For this my tear of guilt fell to the earth."

Tria was greatly moved by her father's experience of the barren rock. He then spoke of Joy and The Last, who he had once encountered as he healed from the ripping of stag horn and Versa hunted for them both.

Listening to him Tria's heart began to soar. She realized she was not alone in her emptiness and rejection. The great Arn, too, had cried a wolf-tear that chilled the earth. But he now lived The Wolf Ways and with them the idyllic life of the wolf pack. Deep in her wolf-heart Tria suddenly remembered the murderous contempt she had for him. She now recognized how this most Magnificent One accepted and treated Bord. She could not help but turn away from her father in embarrassment.

Seeing Tria demure, Arn again spoke, "My daughter, of all the wolf virtues you have learned, remember tolerance must be within a wolf-heart to reach greatness and promulgate The Wolf Ways. Without it, the others will not stand." Arn stared into Tria's eyes and told her it was the only lesson that remained for her to complete.

He went on. "Tria, prosperity could be expanded to our entire species but only by reaching those who would learn The Wolf Ways and keep them. These lone wolves worthy of The Wolf Ways would also need to expand to new lands and adapt to varied prey. Some would not be so inclined, and they hold responsibility for their own decisions. The power of The Wolf Ways would be obvious to all, but for some, bitterness and self-pity would end in meaningless strife and failure."

Again, Tria looked away as her very being was flush with self-indignation, convicted in her heart of her selfishness and self-pity.

Arn insisted: "Only you Tria, the ghostly wolf legend, could be the dominating mentor to many hate-filled lone wolves. Only you have Versa's and my genetics. Only you have the necessary strength and cleverness. Most important-ly, only you can teach The Wolf Ways."

By saying this he acknowledged again it was Tria who was the true author of The Wolf Ways. Receiving this credit from her father at this time gave her comfort to counteract some of the remorse she also felt.

Arn continued explaining: "Only you know the utter des-olation of a lonely spirit and yet also joyously met The Last after banishment. Only you and I, my great daughter, know these two opposites." He insisted further: "This life of the wolf pack proves that you do not have to be a victim of the acts and attitudes of others; you only need to find the joy within and hold yourself to The Wolf Ways to find happiness and greatness."

He asserted further, "You are the one all fear because of the destruction you leveled on our enemies. With Fic at your side, the lone wolves will surely hesitate to attack, but may instead listen. Fic will know when true danger is imminent."

Tria felt as if a great weight had been lifted from her back as this two-wolf Council ended. Then, as the moon broke above the horizon and he saw the bloody glow of Tria's stained fur in the soft moonlight, Arn knew his plan just might work.

22

Arn and Tria returned to a highly-curious pack. All observed a strut of confidence they had not seen in Tria since before she was first banished from the pack. She approached Versa in a submissive posture and received a look of deep understanding from her mother, a tender greeting absent since the time of her rebellious call for Council. Versa realized that Arn had reached their daughter.

Tria turned from her mother's greeting and looked for Fic, approached him and wagged her tail, perhaps a bit more than he had ever seen her do before. In fact, she wagged her tail as if her back end might wiggle off her front. Acceptance can be a mighty thing, and when unconditional, it can be deeply meaningful to the one receiving it and to the one giving it.

Arn and Versa quickly switched to the practical. Versa spoke to her pack: "All that lay behind us is no longer deserving of wolf focus—only a way to guarantee the future of our species needs our attention." Of course, in this regard, Versa served as an integral part of the planning. While Tria knew few details of the plan, she had the look of satisfied confidence that made all the others excited but unsure of what to think. All knew something was afoot and that suddenly, again fully accepted, Tria's role was greatly important.

Some of the loyal five were playing omega dog with Casso, nipping at her, bowling her off her feet and showing their teeth. The weakest in our species is often treated this way. But Tria simply walked into their cruel circle ordering the others, "knock it off!" and they dispersed. She growled at Casso, who immediately showed her loins in submission. Tria did not nip or hover over Casso but showed her a slight tail wag after receiving submission, which lifted Casso's spirits. She intensely desired Tria's acceptance.

All wolves being well-fed and without need for a twilight hunt, they settled down, and Casso returned to the green, pest-free bed prescribed to her by Tria, who found a spot between her and Fic. Jett settled near his beloved Ellip, who kept a watchful eye on Tria.

We wolves do not worry about things yet to come as you do. Certainly, we don't understand why you worry. Some time ago, my human pack leader took a Dale Carnegie class. You know, one of those self-help, positive attitude experts who you hope will make your life better by just paying for their books or lectures. Anyway, ever since the class he loves to say, "Today is the tomorrow you worried about yesterday." We wolves agree; worry is foolish.

We live in the moment, but we are always aware of the potential of change; our defenses are never more than a twitch away from activation. We live in the moment and accept what is, while we are always prepared for what might be next. This is why we test our alphas, why we allow our curiosity to move us to investigate much, and why we nap often. Not to worry is a most sensible way to approach life.

At the wolf camp all slept well that night, and the infestation of fleas that plagued Casso her entire but short life found her evergreen bed most inhospitable. Her new prosperity must be obvious to all the lone wolves if Arn and Versa's plan was to work. She, the starving young offspring of Ket the Elder, would certainly have notoriety if suddenly found to be flourishing. And her brother, Bord, the other survivor of Ket, was becoming quite the majestic and powerful wolf. For the lone wolves would certainly notice Casso's healthy coat, which few of them ever enjoyed, and Bord's impressive health and size was most obvious.

Casso needed some time to gain muscle and strength, so the alpha's plan was delayed. Her poor nutrition delayed the progress of her skeletal growth, but the ample food of the wolf pack would be consumed just in time, before her growth plates might have been stifled to permanent infirmity.

Days, then weeks were spent with Fic replacing Bord in the loyal five. Arn, Versa, Jett, and Bord provided training for Casso, with Bord's efforts focused on the hunt. She would need to learn The Wolf Ways and embrace their overwhelming importance. Tria kept a close eye on their teaching but also could not resist keeping a suspicious eye on this outsider. She had clearly heard her father say that Casso and Bord posed no threat but still harbored reservations. One day Arn spoke to Casso as she walked back into the camp after an evening of twilight hunting lessons. She was shocked as their great leader approached her and gently said, "My hope and dream for you, little one, is that one day after our great triumph, your life might include finding a mate and starting your own pack."

Casso bowed with embarrassment that she should receive such generous wishes and replied to Arn, "Should I gain nothing more than these weeks I have enjoyed with you and The First Wolf Pack, I should count myself most fortunate. You have taught me optimism and gratitude, which brings happiness and peace. Thank you."

Pleased with her response, he wagged his tail—a distinct honor for the omega bitch to receive from the alpha wolf. Arn knew in his heart that she faced much danger, so his wish for little Casso would only succeed if the plan worked well enough for her to survive.

Arn and Versa knew that Casso's skills matched the assignment they had planned for her when they observed her showing gratitude to the original pack; for loyalty cannot sprout within a wolf's heart unless gratitude resides there first. She gladly accepted her place as the omega wolf, and they observed how she was also bonding with Ellip. One day Ellip allowed Casso to enter the inner recesses of the den, and after much smelling and looking, she walked out with an inspired look. Even Ellip, having seen how Tria treated Casso well and how she clearly was now under the control of Arn and Versa, began to take breaks from the care of the jumble litter—at least as long as Arn, Versa, or Jett was in the camp.

As the plan of The Magnificent Ones progressed, Versa took Tria aside to direct her in her first task.

"Tria, you must help the others understand the loneliness you have experienced. You have my permission to explain to the others what up until now only you and Fic have heard from Arn. Take them to the barren rock and share with each the details of how I was inspired to speak the first Wolf Way—cooperation." Tria remembered the words first spoken by Versa, "For you and I both must live, if one is to live."

Tria did exactly as instructed. One at a time, she had them step onto the rock of desolation. Each sprung off it immediately, reacting with fear, confusion, and heartache. After all had tasted the immense depth of emptiness, she explained what an incredible gift they enjoyed—that is, to have a pack—how Arn and Versa battled to near death and then miraculously saved each other.

Because of the painful lesson of the rock, each wolf was intellectually and emotionally primed for imprinting. It especially made the story of the great battle of Arn and Versa indelible. With much charisma she recited The Wolf Ways, which shocked the others, as Tria represented the most vicious of wolves. As she concluded the lessons at the rock, Tria emphasized that sharing The Wolf Ways with other wolves could be the salvation of their entire race. The plan was in phase two.

23

While Casso had to learn to hunt, Bord was not the most effective teacher. However, whenever the entire pack was together, she sought out and found a perfect mentor in Fic. His hindquarters fully healed, he approached Tria instead of the alphas to gauge the reasonableness of his planned request. He then asked her for her opinion.

"Tria, might the alphas allow me to replace Bord and teach the young Casso? Bord does not object."

Tria simply looked at Fic and said, "Ask it and then you shall do it." She was right, the alphas listened and did not object as they noticed wise leadership sprouting up in their daughter.

Fic patiently allowed Casso to develop wolf-pack speed. He did not rush her but pushed her to near exhaustion day after day while always encouraging her. Sometimes Tria joined the two of them, giving young Casso encouragement and sometimes advice on her techniques. Fic's sensitive nature offered him insight into how much pressure she could take without breaking her spirit. Casso's progress accelerated the week Fic and Tria played wolf-tag with her. Fic turned to Tria after one very exhausting game and said, "Never did I imagine you would play wolf-tag with anyone but Jett. You have done a wonderful thing, Tria."

But refusing to reply, the great she-wolf just strutted away, leaving Casso and Fic smiling with satisfaction.

Soon Casso was able to lead the pack in bringing down her first large herbivore. After a meager life hunting raccoon, rat, mole, beaver, marmot, mouse, nuts, and insects, she now not only would eat well, she would provide for the others, including the jumble of growing pups.

She was allowed the honor of dragging the carcass of her first large prey into the wolf camp and presenting it to Arn and Versa, who ate first. They beamed at the strength young Casso had acquired because of their patience, the encouragement of Tria, and the insightful coaching of Fic. Tria ate next, and then all the others scrambled for their fill. Casso watched with a new emotion, a feeling of wolf pride at contributing to the prosperity of the others, and as the omega she ate last, just after Bord. Tria watched this one's growing capabilities and successes, yet never let Casso out of her sight. Fic wondered if his sister was taking the little one under her wing or scheming to keep the potential enemy close by design.

Versa gave Arn the look that said it is time for us to Council. As he moved toward her, she announced to the pack, "Your days of participating in the Wolf Council of The First Wolf Pack are over."

None even hinted at disappointment at their decision. She and Arn injected the deepest respect into their pack with the physical cues of their postures, their stares, and the smell of their physical superiority. Such was their respect that even if they be given a special invitation to a future Wolf Council, none might have assumed they had any right to it. The alphas walked away toward the rock of desolation, and all the wolves knew to remain in the camp.

This time, Versa spoke The Wolf Utterance with such power that the far-off jumble of now 23-week-old pups ran for the den. It is said that the ground shook when Versa meant business. She called the Council, and it began with her youngest offspring and grandpups all shuddering. Casso began to panic, sprinting to-and-fro in the camp with no true direction or purpose. She had never heard the call to Council.

Annoyed by Casso's frantic insecurity, Tria leaped to her feet and knocked Casso down as she was about to pass by the third time. Tria then stood over Casso letting all the others know that only one wolf would be in charge when the alphas were at Council. At this, Ellip, who was in her usual place near the entrance of the den, slowly moved closer to Jett. Tria, seemingly now slipping again into her old ways, void of the self-examination made during the recent private Council with her father, locked her stare upon Ellip to let her know she too was under her domination. Jett with his ineffably confident attitude got up and filled the distance to Ellip, standing between her and Tria to reassure that not even the mighty Tria would threaten his mate and pups.

Tria, as you probably realize, had what you call a short fuse. Quicker than a hummingbird's wings she hurdled over the entrance to the den in one giant leap and placed herself just inches from Jett's muzzle. All the wolves feared what was about to happen, just as Arn and Versa returned. Knowing that their number-one daughter was again exhibiting problem behavior, Versa and Arn strode to her, one on each side, and locked their alpha stares upon her. Tria submitted. Arn gave Tria a knowing look of his disappointment, and Tria looked away. Then Arn took a position on a high place, the rock adjacent to where previously he and Casso reached their understanding.

Then he spoke to them all. "Our race has reached a point of no return. A choice between disaster and prosperity is upon us. Versa and I fear the way of the lone wolf will likely be the future. But we may have one hope. It will only be by the efforts of Tria, Fic, Bord, and Casso that our Wolf Ways may survive. These whom we shall call our "favored four" will bring all that is needed to maximize the chances the wolf pack might survive. But our beloved Tria, while improving, has not yet learned how to control her poisoned blood with wolf-tolerance and wolf-discernment."

Arn repeated this again, but publicly called her beloved, a truly special description for an alpha wolf to give. He did this since he knew of his daughter's continuing struggles, therefore wishing to keep her internal conflicts alive while she was in the presence of the entire expanded pack for support. Fic quietly moved toward Tria until he could once again make physical contact in a reassuring way. Remembering how his contact comforted her and his ability to understand her, she could not help but wonder if he was the wolf of whom Arn spoke, the one able to see into the hearts of others.

Arn continued, "Unfortunately, Casso has brought me word that the lone wolves led by Ket the Elder have proposed a pact with many venomous creatures to overtake our camp, starting with the pups' den. That is why our plan will begin tonight while the chill of night slows their progress toward us."

Pausing for a moment he continued, "Fic, you are much more wolf than you may realize. Your power is only surpassed by your special wolf instinct. It was your kind heart that caused you injury to your hindquarters. Physically you could have protected yourself without injury if you would have gotten your fighting blood up at the moment of attack. You must never hesitate again when there is a mortal threat; others will be counting on you for their very existence. And you must not doubt your special instinct either. When either one is called for, you will know what to do."

Then Arn addressed the two newest members of The First Wolf Pack, "Bord and Casso, you have earned your right to be part of this pack by your obedience, loyalty, and ability to learn and execute The Wolf Ways. You have grown in strength and wisdom beyond what any lone wolf has ever known. Tria will lead this, our favored four, to the boulders west of Jett's hill. They are greater than the boulders of our camp and of those at the stream near the barren rock."

"Tria, you are the perfect twin of your mother, the great Versa. You are young and unwise but with each day I see you gain wisdom. If this pack and The Wolf Ways are to survive you will need to grow into your mother's paws without delay or error. Because you are our offspring, you can do it and you must."

And to the rest of the pack, he said "We will move to Jett's hill by moonlight so that as the morning sun warms the venomous creatures enough for their attack, they will find this place empty. Death will await them. We will all be ready to join our favored four in battle should the need arise. Now, you my loyal five, will lead the way to Jett's hill in a grouping that looks like the peregrine falcon's wings on its dive. Jett and Ellip will follow with the pups. Versa and I will be last and protect the group from rear assault."

With that statement, Arn stepped off the boulder. Fic quickly looked at his sister Tria and quietly told her, "You are ready to do what The Magnificent Ones demand of you. I will be at your side should you need me. I will never abandon you."

24

As the clan of wolves clamored among themselves looking for meaning and insight into what was to happen next, Versa jumped onto the great boulder and ordered the favored four to stand before her with perfect wolf attention. Tria arrived first, then the others. With wolf-focus they locked their entire attention on their alpha bitch, using the entirety of their senses needed for this moment, their eyes, ears, nose, and intellect. Like a border collie being teased with a ball in a hand, never missing the prize no matter how often the human hand faked this way and that, the four stared and listened so intently that nothing could distract them.

Versa then addressed the entire pack: "You will all depart in the order Arn has described. These four will remain with me for explanation of their roles. Start now."

Quickly all the wolves fell in line, pups now able to follow on their own. Versa continued: "Casso you will use your knowledge of the territories of the lone wolves to lead the group to a place so vulnerable but strategic that none will expect to see you there. Fic, you will stay at her side to protect her and show that this little one is now part of The First Wolf Pack. Tria and Bord, you will follow behind and protect their flank. Upon reaching the surprising position in the midst of the lone wolves, you will run to the giant boulders near Jett's hill. Tria, you will call out to us that the chase has begun. Mounting the boulders, you will defend yourselves with reason and the wisdom of The Wolf Ways. Tria, all will fear you and listen to you but may not believe you. Use the other three to complete a message of peace and prosperity available to all. This is all the instruction we have time for, so you must be on your way."

Arn and Versa left their home following the rest to Jett's hill. The three others looked to Casso to act, but she needed a little motivation to lead, so Tria provided it with a bite on her backside. Casso took off toward the back of the boulder and thicket, cutting between and under dense undergrowth including thorns and briars so thick they pulled hunks of fur from the others.

With barely a scratch to her now luxurious fur, Casso's smaller size and quickness allowed her to set a pace that the larger wolves struggled to maintain. At times the forest and thicket were nearly impenetrable such that keen wolf eyes had trouble seeing much in front of their noses, each now scratched and bleeding. None knew just how fast and agile Casso could be in this dense forest, and they would have been impressed if they were not so focused on keeping up with her. She had gained vitality with her now well-fed and maturing body. Covering untold miles in a wood too thick for large beasts, they heard the call of great owls and the screeching of bats' radar as darkness deepened. It is unfortunate that you cannot hear this bat sound since it is unlike anything else in the forest or field.

Soon Casso stopped near the very end of the dense riparian wood allowing the others to catch up to her and come to her side. Tria and Bord, realizing their mistake, quickly retreated to bring up the rear as Versa had previously directed. With their superior vision, they all looked out to an almost endless field of vetch and rye grass flowing over rolling terrain. Now the group was not certain of their location or exactly what direction pointed to Jett's hill, but Casso knew. Soon she was slowly leading them along the edge of the wood to where its roots touched a noisy and roiling river.

They remained there, very still, until they were certain there were no sights, sounds, or smells of lone wolves nearby. Casso whispered, "The direction of retreat will be away from the setting moon, across the field before us. Then we will come upon a narrow canyon. It shall protect our flanks as it leads to Jett's boulders."

Her plan was brilliant, with an impenetrable forest to one side and a wide rushing river to another, they were protected from those two directions as no wolf attack could be fashioned out of those barriers. On the other hand, their retreat as well was limited to only half of the field. Fic looked at her and felt tremendous respect. This once emaciated little one had become a pint-sized powerhouse with incredible agility, speed, and cleverness. He also sensed her great bravery, which fortified his spirit. We wolves and humans of stout heart share many things, not the least important of which is the emotion of fear, but more important is our ability to make the decision to be brave in spite of it. This is part of what has bound us together for eons.

As the sunrise was a couple of hours away and lone wolves would be hunting rodents in the tall grass, Casso said, "It is time." She boldly stepped into the field with Fic at her side. This newest member of The First Wolf Pack was using all her wolf-fortitude to stifle the fear that gnawed at her. She tried not to think about the risks they faced and the critical nature of their assignment. She refused to allow her mind to focus on failure and fear. She fortified herself with the gratitude she felt for her good fortune of being accepted by these great wolves.

Tria told all "make no effort at stealth" as the first two exited the forest. Following just a few yards behind them as instructed, Tria and Bord exited the wood remaining always slightly behind them but not far enough to make the leading pair vulnerable to attack. Now conspicuous in the open plain, with the illumination of the setting moon, Tria appeared again as if she was a glowing bloody-red wolf spirit.

Casso knew the territory so well she could aim them toward a distant dry creek bed that had its origin in the canyon. It would aid their defense and retreat. This natural drain would end at the boulders. She led them slowly, carefully gauging how much time they would have to retreat once the lone wolves massed into a hateful gang. And it worked. As the first morning light barely peaked from the horizon, the four found themselves with at least fifty wolves converging. Casso looked again to Tria, who gave the group direction with a great growl that startled all within the range of her voice. The dark red glowing fur of her head, neck, and chest seemed to expand with the sound. She did it a second time, and with that Bord stepped to the front of the group showing his massive teeth. Tria now had an ally in intimidation when suddenly Fic let out a growl that shook even Tria. At fifty against four, bravery is a decision irrespective of fear.

With this superlative display of the language of wolf dominance, all the lone wolves had second thoughts about attack. Tria directed Casso to lead the way to the boulders. She calmly insisted, "Do not run or trot, but walk confidently as if we own this place too." When only a quarter of a mile from the boulders, the gang of lone wolves could contain itself no longer, and they accelerated to full speed in the blink of an eye. Tria yelled to them, "Now!" And off the quartet went. It was now a race to the boulders, with the fast leading the slow. But then what?

25

None of the favored four had ever approached Jett's hill from this direction, and they did not realize just how far it still was from their reinforcements. Remembering Versa's instruction, as the chase began Tria first stopped long enough to howl their status to the rest of the pack. While running, they all heard Jett's reply: "Message received, but Versa and Arn never arrived."

With a cloud of snapping, snarling wolves on their tails the four reached a stand of sheer rock dominated by a single boulder of immense height. From a grand existence of hunting the largest prey and having more power to jump than other wolves, Tria, Fic, and Bord successfully propelled themselves upward in a seemingly impossible feat. Casso's leap fell short, and she tumbled to the base of the great rock. Instantly Fic dove from his safe perch into the mass of lone wolves and began to defend the courageous and clever little one. Showing the domination Arn predicted, he cast off all comers with strength and speed. With the great rock to their backs and Fic displaying heretofore unseen ferocity, he and his feisty partner soon dispatched the first wave of attackers. A great growl erupted from Tria. All the wolves and all the creatures of the meadow and the forest stopped immediately.

Tria spoke: "I am Tria, the she-wolf who cannot be defeated and I wear the dried blood of many as my crown. Fourteen of your kind have I vanquished in one day with nary a scratch." She continued: "You see with us now two lone wolves who prosper. They are here because we wish this for all."

While Tria was speaking, with immense effort Casso cocked her four legs like a miniature catapult and launched herself toward the rocky platform, scratching and clawing on its side as her jump fell just short. Tria reached down in one easy motion at the apex of the little one's leap and grabbed Casso by the neck to finish her ascent. Fic jumped in unison; the favored four were now safe from attack, but also surrounded by countless enemies with no retreat. Jett, Ellip, and the loyal five were far off, and Arn and Versa were unaccounted for.

Bord spoke next: "The great Arn found me spying on him and Versa. He took my neck to kill me. I could do nothing in the face of his power. Versa stopped him, and they took me into their pack, teaching me to prosper. Some of you may remember me as Bord of the trout stream, skinny but athletic.

See me now. I am larger and more powerful than you. I am well-fed and my coat gleams with health."

Then Casso spoke: "I was dying from starvation when Arn leaped upon me, placing his great jaws upon my throat, but he did not kill me. He inhibited his bite, yet not allowing me to resist. When he released me, as I cowered on the ground beneath him, I spoke of our hunger, me and all of you. He allowed me to take food after all the others in his pack had eaten. The great Tria and this one, Fic, then taught me how to hunt larger game and do many things I never dreamed of doing, things all of you can do someday too. You can see me now even as I grow larger and stronger under a coat of luxurious fur."

The objections of the lone wolves created a din too great to imagine, certainly hurting every wolf's sensitive ears. Why were the lone wolves not listening with interest to the testimony of two such excellent representatives? The verbal vitriol grew in intensity and volume as they found Bord and Casso's testimony unmoving. The bitter howling of the unconvinced echoed off the cliffsides, amplifying the painful protestations until Tria could take no more.

It was then that Tria spoke a second time, bellowing with deafening volume: "I know of the barren place, the rock of desolation." Silence fell upon the riot. "Yes, my heart knows abandonment and emptiness, even more than yours. For I had membership in The First Wolf Pack until my immaturity and ignorance caused me to elevate myself and challenge the great Arn and Versa. Although they had taught us all these new ways, my heart was fixed on dominating the direction of the pack and of all that exists rather than subordination to ones called the alphas. It was then they banished me from their pack."

Again, jeers arose in lone wolf disbelief. "Only mortal combat could have settled your challenge," howled one wolf.

Another yelled out "Banished and now you run with them again? Bollocks!"

Bord somehow amplifying his voice above the disbelieving racket spoke again: "Tria speaks wolf-truth. You knew me in my miserable existence. Had I not wandered too near The Magnificent Ones, I would likely have perished from starvation. If Tria was not in earnest, surely Arn and Versa would have killed me. But you must understand, these two great wolves have discovered something heretofore unknown. It is tolerance." Somehow Bord's second speech attenuated the loud objections of the crowd as he asked, "Why would I be here now if it were not as the great Tria says?"

Tria noticing the softening volume of hate and ignoring their objections then said, "We shall be one race from this point forward. Will you join me in prosperity?"

The slowly-rising sun to her back, perched upon their igneous dais, Tria commanded attention as if some enchantress. With the others at her side looking formidably fit, the crowd of lone wolves began to focus on the impossible—The First Wolf Pack also knew desolation.

Then the sensitive but powerful Fic stepped to the edge of the great boulder in front of the others silencing their murmurs. He gazed out upon the crowd of wolves, but said nothing, seeing their weak bodies and mangy fur. Fic seemed to look into the eyes of each lone wolf, studying them like a great eagle studies the flicker of scales under the ripples of waves as it soars above the waters. Nothing avoided his penetrating stare.

He then called out in grand communication, "Arn, Versa, hear me. It is I, Fic. There are some who are ready and there are others who are not. What would you have us do with these?"

The lone wolves were stunned. For countless moons they had heard Jett's howls at night but did not understand them nor the replies from the others of The First Wolf Pack. But with Fic, many understood, and they began to quarrel among themselves: "How is it that we understand this one?"

Then Arn's great baritone voice replied from a distance, and Fic translated it for the hostile audience.

"All who wish to prosper may join us here at this spot on the next full moon." He continued, "The venomous creatures have been eliminated from the first wolf camp."

Upon hearing this, there were certain lone wolves who could no longer look into the staring eyes of Fic and some slowly sulked away. Again, he fixed his gaze upon all that remained and knew now for certain that many had been moved and many others had not. Yet, there was no way to know if it was safe to descend from the rocky fortress. Would those not moved to curiosity or seeking salvation be too large a number to permit the retreat of the favored four?

With this final communication, nothing more needed to be said. Tria directed her squad to recline and rest upon their unreachable sanctuary until she could plan their next steps. Some of the lone wolves so moved by what had just occurred mimicked the favored four and themselves settled down to rest. The entire atmosphere in the canyon had changed from hatred to calm optimism as the last of the malcontents left the canyon.

26

Jett and the others waiting at Jett's camp heard the exchange between Fic and Arn, but there was no instruction in it for them. It was up to Jett, the other younger alpha male wolf, to lead the second pack and its five guests. Jett wasted no time in exercising his dominance. It was time to hunt again, and it was time to ensure the safe return of his beloved sister and her regiment. Both things could be done in one great and clever effort he reasoned. He selected two to remain with Ellip. He would lead the rest as the rescue expedition.

As the sun reached its apex Jett called to Tria, "At dusk, we will drive prey along the impenetrable forest's edge toward the great river, then scatter the herd of beasts in all directions. You shall take no action until then. Those animals that enter the canyon of the dry stream bed you will take."

All four wolves understood. By instinct, most of the great beasts would avoid the cliffs. They would be frightened by

Jett's pursuit, but only a few would run into the natural funnel of rock. It would be more than the pack would need. While the majority of the frantic beasts would run helter-skelter in all possible directions upon the plain, the lone wolves would be unable to resist chasing a prime meal. Today's messengers would then be free to leave their lofty perch, gather food, and join Jett's expeditionary force.

As evening fell and the herbivores became active, many thundering hooves could be heard. The lone wolves chased about chaotically—many interfering with one another, as they did not know how to hunt together—and a few of Jett's prey ended up in the canyon of the rocky drain. He and the others converged upon the great rock as the favored four were found there with ample food taken, Tria in control. She then barked orders to Jett, "Show us the most direct path back to your camp."

With great admiration and a little amusement, he prompt-ly instructed them all to follow him to his home as he led the way. Even though now an alpha himself, he did not mind following the direction of his cherished sister. With a com-bination of joy at their reunion and relief for the ability to return to the rest, they enthusiastically dragged their quarry to Jett's camp.

As the successful teams arrived, they found Arn and Versa alertly resting above the entrance to Jett's den and the jum-ble of pups. All was secure. Ellip effusively greeted Jett and

Tria, knowing they had succeeded in both the invitation to the lone wolves and in the combination hunt-rescue. Ellip, usually reserved, stepped onto a mound of earth above her brood's den and addressed the entire group.

"This day all has changed for the wolf. I now recognize the absolute brilliance of the plans conceived by Arn and Versa. And I know now the true power of The Wolf Ways. I also am awed by Jett's clever plan to safely bring home the favored four with a masterful hunt. I am privileged to be part of this pack. Let us feast and rest for our propitious future awaits."

Later that evening as all reclined with full bellies and basking in their successes, Versa explained how she had enlisted the help of certain weasels and birds of prey to help eliminate the venomous creatures.

"I sought out a very large and shabby owl that roosted regularly near our camp. I told him that we were discovering new and beneficial ways which some of our race did not understand and for which they wished to kill us. I told the wise bird our enemies had allies. They would attempt the next day, a surprise attack by venomous creatures. I knew the owl enjoyed these despicable reptiles as prey. The bird stared at me for a few moments but said nothing until he blinked his soulful eyes, appearing to nod his acceptance. With that I saw him swoop to the ground many yards away from me and engage in conversation with a clan of stone martens. It was then I knew for certain he had accepted my request."

Versa held their rapt attention as she continued. "While the favored four were upon the grand boulder, Arn and I had remained hidden nearby to guard Jett's hill. The weasels and birds were grateful for learning about the swarming of food at a time when it could be safely taken. Upon the despicable arrival of the hired assassins at the warmth of midday, the venomous creatures would find nothing. They would slither their way around the camp looking for the promised spoils told them by Ket the Elder, but would find none. They would slither from rock to pit to tree trunk in desperate search for the promises made until the coolness of the evening slowed their bodies. The great eagle owls and the small carnivorous mammals would overtake them with ease as their bodies cooled."

The helpful predators knew that Versa would never lie, so they gladly planned to encircle the wolf camp without fear and observe at a distance the scaled demons as they found nothing to eat. And more importantly, they knew the legend of Ket the Elder, with his insidious and hypnotizing lies he just might be evil enough to deceive even snakes.

Many questions were asked, until Arn grew impatient. He looked to his precious Versa, and she knew his mind. Although it was late, Versa decided to again call an expanded Council. All stopped where they stood as The Wolf Utterance was spoken and the pups desperately sought shelter. Versa first addressed her pack: "All of you have shown great courage and intelligence today. Your success was only possible by all of you working together. Our species will forever remember what you did this day. Tria, you have made me especially proud for you chose to reach the lone wolves with more than your formidable power. Now with this behind us, there is much more that must be done."

With that, Arn stood front and center and Versa stepped aside. He continued, "My pack, our plan is simple. All lone wolves present at the dry creek bed when the moon is next full will first be observed from a distance. I, the great Arn, can smell a liar, a faker, or a deceiver. Those assigned as sentries will stand on the cliffsides at the entrance to the canyon at its apex. Tria shall stand upon the great rock, and Fic will join her there. As I pinpoint the stench of any traitors, the sentries are to chase them from the gathering. Tria and Fic will tell of The Wolf Ways to those who remain."

Thankfully, thought Arn as he gazed upon Tria, his most special one had become the Dean of The Wolf Ways. His wolf-heart ached at the pain he and Versa had caused Tria to endure when they banished her. But he realized that had her rebellious call for Council been accepted, she would not be the great creature she had become. Certainly, her suffering brought her much closer to the lone wolf and offered her the ability to perhaps reach them.

Versa now stepped forward to finish the business of the Council. "We only have a few days to study and rehearse.

All will study The Wolf Ways at Tria's feet, even those given responsibilities as sentries. Casso, however, will be a spy, traveling throughout the land of hills looking for conspiracies to derail peace and other plots of which only she and I know, and shall not be shared. Only she is agile, clever, and brave enough to work behind enemy lines. Jett and Ellip will remain in charge of all the pups. Arn and I will direct all activities and interject if needed." Casso stood in stunned silence as she learned of her critical role in such a public way.

With that, the alphas ended the Council. Earlier that evening as they completed their banquet, all the wolves had thought that the hardest parts were behind them but now they began to wonder what else lay ahead.

On its east side facing the mountains, Jett's camp provided a natural amphitheater, which Tria used to perfection. She drilled all the others as Arn and Versa watched: "For you and I both must live, if one is to live—which is pack cooperation and loyalty. The dominance of the alpha, inhibited bite, tolerance, discerning real threats, only alphas mate, shunning, the omega wolf, and the den, the use of wind direction, angle of attack, stealth." Tria demanded, "Repeat them. Tell me again what each means. Explain why it is important. Explain what is in it for the individual wolf."

Tria worked them hard day after day, but she also understood our wolf attention span is short and our need for exercise is inescapable. So Tria would give them many breaks for naps and time off to play or hunt. And this great professor of The Wolf Ways realized from Versa's story, the killing of the venomous creatures was only possible because the eagle owls and small predators believed Versa would not lie. So, Tria explained to her pupils that all the Wolf Ways she taught are not sustainable and truly effective if you are not always truthful. Only Tria had the authority to add to The Wolf Ways. She offered this, the last message to her students as her lessons wrapped up: "No untruth or deception could ever be allowed within those who practice The Wolf Ways for if ever built upon even the smallest lie, all will crumble. We wolves do not and must not lie."

The members of The First Wolf Pack, both the born and adopted, embraced all Tria's teachings. Now with schooling behind them each thought this was a simple, one-step plan of just teaching The Wolf Ways at a complete and precise level to the lone wolves. They felt well-equipped and wondered how many times the lessons would have to be repeated to be absorbed by lone wolves. The members of The First Wolf Pack teaching corps expected they would train their students in small groups to maximize learning. Each lone wolf would get more attention this way, they reasoned.

What they did not know—but Arn, Versa, and Tria, did— is that words may teach, but only experience fuses concept to reality in a profound and unforgettable way. For a wolf, without reality of practice, concepts are of little use.

As all the student teachers had prepared well and there was no need for further rehearsal, Versa told Fic and Tria to join Arn for one more remote lesson. He led them the great distance back to the original wolf camp and to the barren rock, the rock of desolation he helped create. Arn stood upon it declaring, "Fic, you, too, will stand here so you will know that this is our future if you doubt The Wolf Ways and fail in your mission." Then he stepped off.

You'll recall that Fic had watched his sister linger and collapse upon the rock and afterward he had sniffed it, but he never stood upon it. He had felt the transmission of misery jump through the air by the mere hovering of his paw. But he did as instructed. And with that Arn had to pull Fic off the rock of desolation as its emptiness so devastated him, this most sensitive of wolves.

Arn waited for Fic to recover as he addressed them, "Tria, you know this desolation as you, too, helped create it. Fic, now you also understand what is at stake. You now also have a better glimpse into your magnificent sister. Because of this you will be able to reach the lone wolves in their brokenness as only you can." Fic, cut to the quick, now understood what he had seen in Tria's eyes, but previously could not fully comprehend. Then regaining enough strength of spirit, Fic spoke: "My great father and my beloved sister, what emptiness has touched you. The aching in my heart might have taken my very life at the moment you pulled me from its desolation. How is it you both endure this within yourselves?"

Arn looked at his son and spoke with unwavering wisdom. "These things are what they are because of who we are. We are wolves; we fight with tenacity greater than all other creatures. Should we not fight, learn, and grow, then we shall be like those who only know misery and dearth. Should we not place ourselves in the service of the pack, our opportunities to grow shall be scarce. My strength is The Wolf Ways—without them all is folly."

Fic looked at his father, understanding him in a way he never before realized. Only knowing the bounty and joy of the pack led by Arn and Versa, he never imagined that his father could know and overcome such pain. Fic was compelled to reply to his father.

"There is much for which I must be forever grateful. Because of The First Wolf Pack, loyalty shall forever be in our race. May I always make you proud, my father, by following the ways you lived and Tria has taught."

Listening to what Arn said, Tria, too, found herself in deep reflection. All that had transpired swirled in her head—the banishment, The Last, the battles, the realization of her failure when she did not understand Ket the Elder and his compatriots. She pondered how returning to the service of the pack and the loyalty to it made her almost whole again—how the guidance of her sire and the support of her brother

Fic made a difference in escaping the near irresistible bottomless pit of self-pity, ingratitude, and hate.

Now she fully comprehended that she must resolve the others' distrust. She realized she could not be fully ready for the greatness The Magnificent Ones demanded of her until she asked Ellip for her trust and received it. Explaining her recognition of incompleteness to Arn, he praised her for her introspection.

Fic then reassured Tria, "Ellip and Jett will know if you deserve it, when they have enough trust in you that you may play with the pups."

Arn looked at Fic with great admiration for his wise insight into the hearts of wolves.

The three returned to join the rest. Tria went directly to Jett and Ellip and began to tell them of her heart, the desolation of being banished, the restoration given her by The Last, the battles and the eventual re-submission to return to the pack. Ellip, now being supportive, recalled her surprise when Tria provided the frightened Casso with direction—albeit by a tough knockdown—and the time she showed the little one food, drink, and a bed of healing comfort. She recalled Tria's submission to the alphas upon the reunification of the pack, and she had heard rumors about her role in creating the rock of desolation. Ellip looked to Fic, who slowly blinked his eyes, conveying peace.

Jett and Ellip stepped back from the entrance to their den and the jumble of pups swarmed Tria in play. She was now ready.

27

All wolves know when the moon is about to be complete, so there was no need to remind or re-invite anyone. Although for two nights before the propitious time arrived, Jett could not resist offering a serenade to his pack, with messages of hope and confidence in Tria and Fic. With minor accompaniment from Bord, Jett's aria continued until The Last appeared at Jett's camp. All the wolves enjoyed the visit immensely and were reassured that it was the nature of things that wolves should live in packs, with order and loyalty.

They would sleep well this first night and again tomorrow, the day before destiny would play its hand. Joy landed on Tria's great forepaw, flashed a couple times to Tria's delight, then flittered to her right ear and spoke in that soft, almost imperceptible sweet voice.

"You, my princess, have not completed your journeys but never fear, we will be with you to preserve you in your successes. We will never abandon you, even until the end. Your ear into which I speak will remind you of the need for self-control and discernment."

That first night per Arn's orders Casso was to return with the results of her espionage. As all slept, Arn stood on a high spot near Tria's amphitheater awaiting Casso. His heart filled with trepidation because of her tardiness, as he knew this adopted bulwark of courage would never betray her pack, even in the face of death. With only part of the night and the next day remaining and the land so vast, he knew something must be done to find her. Fic awakened sensing trouble in his magnificent sire but lay quietly. Tria was near, and as Fic tried to slowly move his position closer to Arn, she placed a powerful foreleg across his. He knew he could not move, as they both held perfectly still. Fic read his sister's mind as she again pondered the little one's betrayal.

As light barely overcame the dark, all the pack began to rustle. They awoke to see Arn on the same spot he had taken before all had retired. Gathering around him, none knowing when Casso might return, all sensed his uneasiness. Versa looked to Arn with the alpha pair bond, and instantly she leaped to his position as he descended. From above them she spoke, "One of you must find Casso within the enemy's territory. It can only be one, no more. Most certainly you will not survive, so we will not choose who goes. You must gather together without me and Arn to unanimously agree to the rescuer."

Thus, with the participation of the original pack plus Bord and Ellip, a new kind of faux council was held. With no wolf utterance to begin, for surely that would be wolf blasphemy for a non-alpha to make the utterance, they proceeded as directed. As they headed to Tria's amphitheater, their recent classroom and perhaps a perfect place for such a momentous decision, Arn and Versa attended to the pups.

In the reverse order of pack hierarchy, each wolf spoke of their concerns for the pack and for Casso. Bord and the others had little to say. Only Fic, who was just before Jett and Tria, pressed his need to volunteer. He made a convincing case like a skilled barrister saving the life of an innocent. When Jett's turn arrived, he spoke of Ellip and his litter.

Now it was Tria's turn. As she began to speak, she stuttered and paused, struggling to say anything. Fic looked deeply into her eyes and said "Yes Tria, you are certainly the one who must go. I have looked into your heart and you need this chance at final redemption. It is only you with your unequaled knowledge, strength, and viciousness matched with your desire for making all things right, that success has a chance. It is true that you will not cease in your search for Casso until you prove her a traitor or a hero, then kill her or save her. Do I speak wolf-truth, Tria?"

All the other wolves were beyond shocked; they were also terrified that this talk would launch Tria into a lethal frenzy. None had any idea that Tria harbored thoughts of Casso's possible betrayal or that Tria would tolerate such a disrespectful display from Fic. As the tension built, Bord slowly moved away from the group, being unnoticed by the others and their anticipation of bloodshed.

Shocking them all, Tria answered Fic: "All you say is right. You are my brother who sees into the hearts of others." Then she walked back to the alphas leaving the others in stunned silence. With her return, Arn and Versa huddled with Tria, explaining the detailed plans for reconnaissance given to Casso.

28

Tria used the last hour of weakening darkness to find the dense thicket within the forest that she saw swallow up Casso the day she left for spying. Her nose to the ground she picked up Casso's trail and made great distance, driven by a determination to do more than just find the little one, daughter of Ket the Elder. Knowing that time worked against their plans, even at great risk to herself she decided to move while daylight bathed everything in its revealing exposure. Silently she maintained the trail, covering as much ground as she could, hoping not to reveal her presence.

Eventually Tria found herself in a place she had never seen before.

Stands of trees, short and fruitful, were interspersed with taller woody cousins thinly spread high above, so sparingly that light could feed all the leaves below with life. Yet closer to the ground waved tall grass, patches long and thick wherein nothing could be seen, only smelled or heard. It was a perfect trio of high green canopy, fruitful mezzanine, and ground-hugging warren. The trail seemed to end there. But where was Casso?

Using her great hearing, Tria heard the whispers of wolves. With her superior olfactory gift she inhaled the urgent smell of one who fears imminent death. She tried to count the smells, at least thirteen individuals, two of whom seemed familiar.

The alpha's planned for Tria to find Casso with her stealth and then together sneak out of enemy territory. But they also knew in their hearts that Casso's failure to return on time could mean her capture or demise had already occurred. As Tria sensed the wind changing directions, she altered her position to remain undetectable. And in doing so, she smelled the wretched stench of lies and deceit. She knew it was Ket the Elder. That bitter taste returned to her mouth, the one she had experienced when Ket was within her jaws, but she did not kill him. Smell and taste are of the same sensory origin within us. It was time to rescue a comrade or terminate a betrayer. Either way she intended to kill Ket the Elder.

Tria carefully pondered her options—frontal assault with a brazen charge, which would always be first choice, but she also considered how deception might aid her. Tria remembered that time when she might have faced twelve, but reinforcements came to her side. Now she considered how the question of her capabilities might be irrevocably answered. Instead, she remembered the lynx, her right ear, and chose stealth. She contemplated what she had learned about the wind, about vectors, and about the inability of lone wolves to control their rage.

Slowly moving around the place where the key smells centered, Tria began to crawl through the thickest grass with no intention of remaining undetected. As she circled, she could hear Ket tell Casso of her options: "Betray The First Wolf Pack or be slowly killed by venomous creatures. Your time to decide shall not be delayed. Tell us what we want to know or face a horrible death. The venom of these creatures works slowly, painfully, taking days to kill. You shall all the while suffer excruciating pain. You will not be able to move, although you'll wish to take your own life to stop the agony."

The other wolves laughed in sinister unison, excited by the talk of suffering and slow death. They snapped the air in front of Casso's face, spewing taunts of every kind.

Ket continued: "Once bitten your unimaginable suffering will cause you to plead with me for a second chance. I will delight when you beg for mercy, but a second chance will not come. Your pleadings will inform me that not only your body suffers but your entire being has paid a price for defying me."

Hearing this, Tria's rage began to boil uncontrollably. Her pace through the warren of grass grew more anxious, but then she heard Casso speak.

"Ket, you will not terrify me into betraying The First Wolf Pack. They have shown me the better way. Before you kill me, I must offer you a chance to join them at the canyon upon the full moon. As much as I may suffer, you have my answer."

Tria stood there, amazed. She made one last jump from her lush labyrinth to the next while catching a quick view of the evil cabal. Eight wolves formed a circle around Ket the Elder plus three compatriots who held Casso to the ground. Tria knew she must act quickly.

Suddenly, hearing hissing under her feet, Tria looked down at a slithering mass of vipers, and her skin crawled with disgust. But nothing would interfere with her now clear mission. Stepping in front of them to stop their progress she whispered to this swarming group of detestable creatures, "I am Tria, daughter of Arn and Versa. We of The First Wolf Pack do not lie. You are being deceived by the greatest of liars, Ket the Elder. You will not have the food promised, only one wolf whom none of you can consume. Ket only wants you to waste your venom. Some of your kind were deceived by him upon the hill of Arn and Versa. Those were attacked by weasels and owls instead as their bodies cooled." The slithering stopped for a moment while the reptiles considered what was said.

Tria stood unyielding, stifling her fear of their venom. Tria postured herself to exude confidence and control of the situation, she expanded her chest and stared at them all without blinking just as she had seen Versa do to her. The snakes did nothing more. These detestable creatures are masters of lying in wait, unseen until they strike. She could not know for certain, but hoped she had reached them.

With the rustling of grasses and Tria's whispers, the lone partners in terror grew certain a spy was nearby. Four of them, with Ket's permission, began to advance on Tria's position while four others stayed with him. The three binding wolves holding Casso maintained their position as well.

Hidden by the grasses and using her keen nose and acute hearing, she began to dispatch the searchers. One by one she outflanked them. Jumping from grassy maze to maze without detection, each enemy met its quick demise. As sound of the quick battles repeated from place-to-place, Ket knew it must be the ghostly she-wolf that had killed fourteen in one day. The one from whom he had escaped.

While the sound of each hidden battle continued, a wolf burst from the nearby thicket. Charging headlong on a frontal assault against the remaining eight lone wolves, sprang Bord. Jumping into the circle holding his dear Casso, five wolves including Ket attacked him. With three holding Casso, and five against one, Bord held his own, taking down two wolves as he had done in the heavy timber with Tria and Jett. As Tria finished off the last of the four lone wolves pursuing her she accelerated to where Bord still fought.

28

Casso, rescue at hand, broke from their hold and took on the three. First vanquishing one and then quickly a second lone wolf, she turned to fight the third. As she squared off with the last of her captors, looking behind him she watched helplessly while Ket dealt a fatal bite to the neck of Bord before Tria arrived a moment too late.

Tria turned to fight the remaining lone wolves. Finishing her last massacre, she turned to pursue Ket. Sensing their defeat with Tria's power now unleashed upon them, Ket once again looked for an immediate retreat. Casso bravely fought the last wolf while Tria leaped through the air and landed just short of Ket as he sped away.

Stumbling, and then regaining her footing, she raced forward to catch him, to eliminate the one she so despised. At that moment, one venomous creature lurking in the grass sunk its fangs deeply into Ket's hindquarters. Then another bit him upon his foreleg hissing "In retribution for your lies." Then another followed in attacking Ket, deriding him, "This is for our brethren eaten by owls and weasels."

Ket the Elder lay writhing in pain before Tria could exact her final revenge. With seething hate she approached him, staring down at him as the blood of his comrades dropped from her fur into his face. She said nothing. He looked up at her and begged, "Kill me now. Take my throat and rip it open. Tear my head from my body. Show me mercy, oh great one."

One venomous creature looked up at Tria and said, "This one is ours. Do not interfere with our ways."

In emotionless silence, Tria strode away from Ket toward Casso. As they stood victorious on the battlefield observing eleven vanquished adversaries and the single revenge of the venomous creatures, Casso collapsed onto Bord's lifeless body. Tria felt a wolf-tear welling, but she successfully held it back. She looked at Casso and said, "I am a wolf of many faults, the greatest of which was to suspect any betrayal by Bord, he the most loyal of The First Wolf Pack. It was his silent bravery and selflessness that drove him to find you. When all the others were uncertain, he chose courage and loyalty."

Casso sniffed her silent brother and wept bitterly. Many tears fell, not as the single wolf-tear of Tria and Arn, but countlessly they flowed. As they poured from her face and reached the ground, the soil began to erode and soon exposed the rock below. The power of her tears caused the rock to fissure and separate as she stood motionless on the edge. Slowly Tria moved to her adopted sister's side and glanced down into a seemingly bottomless pit. She carefully began to move Casso away from the forming crevasse. Tria feared it might have swallowed up the devastated little one had she not pushed her away.

Moving her to safety, Tria looked to Casso and said, "You are truly of our pack. Your courage and dedication are greater than I imagined. Oh, that I may one day have the loyalty you possess. Forever will your name be known among wolves who live in packs for you have shown me the pure essence of what the pack must be. And so, too, shall the name of Bord be forever remembered, for he did what needed doing with no regard for himself. Because you and I were truly one with him and the others, The First Wolf Pack may yet survive; thank you little one."

Snapped back to reality, Tria said "We have no time to waste. We must return."

As Tria headed off, Casso sprinted into her path redirecting her with a body check and said, "No Tria, I know a better route." And with that Tria followed Casso.

29

On the second night of preparation before the canyon's class, the last night before the full moon, Tria and Casso arrived as Jett's song ended and The Last charmed them with their light. Casso went directly to the alphas and gave her report.

"While many had been moved by Tria's admission to desolation of heart and many others were transfixed by Fic's penetrating stare and his ability to speak to them, some had tried to raise a gang to disrupt the upcoming event. Many malcontents led by Ket the Elder planned to torture me into betraying you. They caught me as I made my last attempt to gather intelligence. They had devised a plan to surround and attack all of us. Ket recruited great numbers of them. They would utilize the canyon as a trap. I was to lead you into a place of no escape. Ket told lies to venomous creatures to gain their cooperation to kill me—a slow and painful end. Yet he would spare me if I would betray all of you. As the horrible creatures drew near to me, I heard wolf battles. I knew it must be the great Tria coming to my rescue. As she fought them one at a time using stealth, Bord suddenly burst from the thicket and attacked the eight that still detained me. He fought valiantly but was blindsided by Ket with a lethal bite. But because of Bord and his brave attack, I was able to break free. Tria burst from the grasses and the rest of our enemies were eliminated." Exhibiting wolf humility suitable for the most loyal pack member, Casso continued: "Tria and Bord saved me and all of you with great courage and strength. I will forever remain in their debt."

Casso then received a welcome worthy of a great hero from the others as they mobbed her with affection. Perhaps this little one had taught the others more about valor than they ever knew, and it was time they praise her and thank her for it, which they did in earnest. Casso chose not to discuss the details of the battle, and Tria respected the hero's wish, all the details of that courageous, historic event would remain between them. She also showed humility by never disclosing that she, the once emaciated one, had vanquished three lone wolves on her own. Perhaps, too, this extraordinary little one also felt some guilt for her inability to fight off more lone wolves and somehow save her brother.

Only many years later would Tria tell her progeny of the pint-sized powerhouse and the adopted one who gave his life, both of whom defined loyalty and courage. Eventually she would spread the story of these true wolf-heroes to many wolves.

30

By our nature, we wolves are not late or early; we are always on time. So, the next evening the wolf-instructors populated the great rock exactly as Arn had instructed. Only lone wolves sincerely in quest of a better life remained after the fakers identified by Arn were dispatched by the sentries. Twenty-one lone wolves filled the small canyon of the dry creek bed, sincerely seeking what the great Arn offered.

Word spread among those gathered of the destruction of the malcontents and how Ket the Elder still writhed in pain among the grasses. The members of The First Wolf Pack could smell the weird combination of fear, hate, and optimism filling the canyon as all became aware of Ket's demise. Then word spread about the death of Bord, who had only recently stood before them to encourage advancement of their species. It was an oddly joyous yet somber mood that filled the air that evening.

As the warmth of the evening sun gave way to the cooling sky, an early moonrise, a full and glorious supermoon ascended directly behind Tria and Fic. The moon, like the sun in their first appearance on the great boulder, beamed behind them, allowing Fic to see into the eyes of all.

Tria and Fic were irresistible. Speaking of The Wolf Ways brought hope to the assembled, eventually being joined by enthusiasm. Tria and Fic went on carefully covering each topic with skillful accuracy, always being certain to include the benefits of each to their eager students. As the others looked on, they all noticed how something had changed in Tria. She exuded her irrepressible strength and knowledge of The Wolf Ways, but there was something new, a heart filled with compassion and a sincere interest in her students.

Tria so profoundly desired all wolves to abandon the ways of the lone wolf; all assembled could see it and feel it resonate deeply within. Her teaching touched those in attendance so deeply, they clamored for more. Fic reached into their innermost wolfenness, inspiring their trust in someone who knew each heart. Cheers rang out praising Tria and Fic. The promising teaching of these two leaders from the original wolf pack motivated and inspired their pupils, but all who remained in the canyon were most intensely moved by the selfless story of the adopted hero, Bord.

Late into the night, Tria and Fic explained The Wolf Ways, and none left or succumbed to distraction. Surely their eloquence and sincerity drove home indelible lessons. As the lecture wound down, the other wolves of The First Wolf Pack wondered why they, too, had to endure the lessons recently taught to them since only Tria and Fic acted as teachers that night.

Suddenly Arn and Versa burst onto the scene, effortlessly jumping onto the boulder to join the instructors. The crowd was transfixed. Many had never seen these two legendary wolves up close, and their stature and presence were awe inspiring. Tria gazed at them in amazement, realizing her parents were even larger and more powerful than ever. Wondering about the purpose of their appearance, Tria and the others would now learn The Magnificent Ones brought a surprise.

No one knew of Arn and Versa's plan in advance. Arn spoke first in a voice that rattled the rocks, causing billows of dust to explode from the small avalanches of pebbles and stones which trickled down the canyon's sides everywhere.

"You lone wolves will be blessed with abundance if you make The Wolf Ways your own. You must not deviate from them, and you must pass them down to every generation. And to all others you shall speak of Bord and his sacrifice."

Then Versa spoke. "I have counted twenty-one of you lone wolves. Individually, seven of our pack will each take three of you to join with them to teach you how to live our ways. Thus, there will be seven tribes of The First Wolf Pack. It is each of you who will guarantee the future of our race. But you must cooperate fully. Do not challenge your alpha, or you will be overwhelmed by their strength. For just as Tria could kill fourteen in one day with nary a scratch, all our offspring have equal power. They will lead you with great honesty, wisdom, and loyalty to your pack. When ready, you will populate distant lands, for as your hunting skills eventually equal ours, these valleys and hills will no longer support all of your needs. Therefore, one pack-in-training will travel to occupy land far south of our hills. The other six groups will travel north, northeast, and northwest. You will hone your hunting skills while you travel to new lands. On your journey, you will find many of your known prey, but as you proceed farther, you will find varied small and large beasts never before encountered. The climate will change, but you will adapt. As you travel you may accept other lone wolves into your group, but only if the alpha sees fit. Mating will occur once your new territory has been reached and a dominant pair is found worthy. Only these alphas may mate. As you reproduce, the strongest, young adult male and female wolves of each litter will be banished, sent out to new and more distant lands. These are your instructions. You will return here tomorrow as the sun begins to rise. After three days of training, hunting, and eating with us upon our lands, you will set forth, never to return."

Now the original pack members finally realized why they all had to endure Tria's lessons. They all stood in stunned silence. But sometimes the best way to lead is to use surprise. Each would be leading a one-way wolf-pack expedition. Their days with The First Wolf Pack were about to end.

Arn then gave final instructions: "Any lone wolf wishing to lead the hunt or eat out of order instead of following our instructions may leave now, for should you disobey during the next three days or on your journey, you will be destroyed. There is no other way."

With that, Arn led his soon-to-be dissolved pack to his camp, informing Jett and Ellip he expected them to lead the seventh tribe. Though they had done well and already lived in the harmony of The Wolf Ways, Arn needed them to relocate further away, to a valley north of the mountains nearest The First Wolf Pack. Only Arn and Versa would retain dominion over their original territory.

31

As the three days of training began, Tria sought out Arn and Versa to express her concerns for the anticipated journeys. The alphas listened intently, amazed at Tria's understanding of dangerous possibilities.

During the three days, Fic was given the responsibility of creating the new mini-packs, the seven tribes of The First Wolf Pack. Did you ever notice how some dogs just seem to like certain dogs and want nothing to do with others? Fic knew who belonged together and who did not. With Tria's successful training of the other members of her pack there was a most desirable ratio of students and teachers. With three days of pack hunting and training complete, Fic had done well. Teamwork incubated in each of the loners from the lessons so well learned from the instructors trained by Tria and, of course, from Fic's matchmaking. The two siblings successfully made this part of the plan work.

Maybe it was her need to fill the departure of her beloved Jett or maybe it was Fic's many qualities, but either way Tria now had a new strong permanent brother-sister bond. Eventually, she would realize Fic's greatest gift was quite literally saving her from self-destruction.

With Tria as his biggest advocate, and because of this obvious success, Fic was directed by The Magnificent Ones to the land to the south. A shorter journey would be his reward. And his group would include a fifth member, Casso. The pint-sized powerhouse of courage and grit had physically grown into quite a compact but powerful wolf.

With this news, Tria found the opportunity to speak with Fic alone. She told him "Casso has chosen not to speak of her ordeal and this must be respected, but I am free to say that she is most loyal and courageous. There is no wolf with a more spirited, sincere, and loyal heart. You are truly fortunate to have her in your pack. Please forgive me for ever having doubted her, but all the while you knew who and what she was; I did not." This was the fourth time Tria had bared her soul—first to Arn, then to Jett and Ellip, then to Casso upon her rescue, now to Fic.

Tria felt as if a massive weight lifted from the innermost essence of herself; her wolf-heart had finally been restored to its natural state of purity. She had been proven wrong about Casso and Bord and now unconditionally admitted such. But it was mostly the sacrifice made by Bord that changed her. How one, not of The First Wolf Pack, but adopted into it, could believe in all its wolf virtues more profoundly than any other wolf thereof made a significant impression on her. She now had a superhero of sorts to emulate and to remind her to never doubt her pack and to never quit regardless of the obstacles before her.

The first day while hunting class was in session under the guidance of Tria, Versa knew that all was in the hands of her most capable and now purified daughter. She told Arn she would soon return. Then Versa left the training grounds and would not be missed as she sought out the great owls that devoured the failed raiders of their camp. When arriving under their roosts, locating that shabby owl who previously helped her, she asked for his flock's help in learning what lay beyond the faces of the distant mountains. He told her they knew not the interior of the mountains, but there was a legend of a great eagle from the lands east. He explained to Versa the details of the legendary bird and told her that he was known to occasionally visit the mountains of which Versa spoke. Perhaps if she found him, he could help her. As she spoke with the small flock and its leader, a few owls first gathered above her, soon many more congregated everywhere about her as if called by some silent message. Suddenly, Versa found herself in a circle of eyes that made her believe their every word—piercing, not like the eyes of Fic, but burning with wisdom and truthfulness. More and more owls arrived, and they encircled her until she could not count their number. A cloud of eagle owls had formed atop the forest canopy so dense, the forest floor upon which she stood seemed to turn dark as a moonless night.

Versa remained motionless as they began to squabble among themselves in a language she did not understand. Then complete and utter silence. One bubo hopped from its perch above her and onto a low branch so close to Versa's face that they must have shared the same breath. The bird then whispered one word. Suddenly, intense squawking erupted as the name was whispered. The entire flock burst from their individual roosts and into the sky in a gigantic hysterical flight of chaos. Feathers beat against feathers as a cloud of birds too thick to fly somehow elevated and cleared the treetops.

The unmoving lone owl who spoke the agitating name told her, "When you get to the mountains, stand near where the river descends from a great height, and there over the din of the falling water, call out his name. Then briefly wait. Call a second time but no more." Her wise little friend then followed the other owls skyward and disappeared from sight.

Versa ran flat out for a day and a night without stopping until she stood in the presence of the behemoths at sunrise. Determination was contained so deeply in the bones and visceral mass of this great wolf, complete exertion seemed not a chore, but a reward—exhaustion ever pursued but never achieved. Such was the spirit of Versa.

The mountains on the east side of her territory ascended to a few snowy summits, but what she saw now appeared beyond intimidating, dwarfing those of her homeland. Mountaintops buried in clouds with massive glaciers on distant peaks beyond, Versa began to doubt. But she recognized there was no room for doubting if her race was to survive. Versa then called the great eagle's name, and then again, a second time: "Periphas . . . Periphas!" She then waited in the deafening sound of the waterfall just described by the owl. Anxiously she waited as it pounded out a thundering rhythm behind her.

With a wingspan that cast a shadow across the morning sun, the great bird soared above for three full circles before landing above her in an alpine spruce that bent toward the earth, now burdened and struggling with his size.

"What do you want of me, earth dweller?" he asked.

"I am Versa of The First Wolf Pack. I am told by the eagle owls to the south that you have seen much of the mountains."

The aviator left his perch and swooped to the ground before Versa. She was amazed at his size. Versa had to look up into his eyes. With wings that might have stretched across Tria's amphitheater, the magnificent creature loomed larger than any bird or animal she had ever seen.

"How did you know my name or how to call to me?" asked the great bird.

Tria replied "The eagle owls of my homeland have found me worthy. They engulfed me in a flock of their kind as large as a cloud, then one spoke to me. I am here because those others of your kind told me you may know much of the endless mountains."

Periphas replied, "Climb upon my back and I will show you what you could otherwise never see. Should you attempt to deceive me, I will drop you to your death."

Versa eagerly jumped up on his back and felt his splendid muscles, rigid and powerful but the giant bird's feathers provided her a secure cushioned place, so long as he did not bank or dive to drop her.

While they began their flight, Versa spoke of how The First Wolf Pack had begun, how her race was in conflict, and how she and Arn planned to save her species. The great eagle listened, enthralled, asking many questions to test her story. She held nothing back.

She did not know that he was once a great king of a distant land before he became an eagle. But he spoke as one possessing great wisdom and intelligence. Versa freely answered his interrogations without fear, for her words contained only truth and honesty. She asked: "Please tell me great bird, how is it that you are so enormous and so wise?"

Ignoring her question, Periphas declared to Versa, "You are who you say, and your story is true. Now your request will be granted, but you must promise to pay me the price I demand."

Versa responded in turn, "What is this price, great bird, and how shall I commit before I know the demand?"

He explained, "As a king I was known for my wisdom and fairness; you will have to trust me. Will you trust me wolf?"

Versa replied, "I know not of your kingdom or throne, but I hear no deceit in your voice and smell no deception on your breath. The eagle owls of my land are forthright and fair, and I do not believe they would deceive me. I will pay your price and honor my promise in every way if you will show me what I must learn."

With that, the great wings pressed against the air beneath them in massive strokes, driving the airborne host higher and higher until they were above even the tallest mountain peak. Periphas then showed the great she-wolf where each of her tribes should cross the mountains, to the east, to the west, and to the north. For all of the remaining hours of daylight they continued to converse while Versa viewed the mountains below from among a peppering of clouds. Periphas left no detail of the landscape unshown or unexplained, until a soft landing ended the day at dusk, precisely upon the spot of the trip's origin.

"How may I repay you for the kindness you have shown me, great one?" Versa asked as an invitation to finally hear his price.

Then Periphas said in reply, "It is for my cousins the eagle owls that you have found my favor, for they would not have given you my name unless you were of similar greatness and honesty."

He continued, "Now, my price. You shall promise me these things: First you shall not repeat my name to any wolf, for it is only in the realm of birds to do so. And your debt shall also include sending your daughter Tria to the ends of the earth to continue what you and Arn have begun. Only this daughter of yours shall not be bound by the confidentiality I demand; she must know all. Only she may speak my name among your race. It shall be good for the inhabitants of my former kingdom that your ways will be spread there. Next, you shall tell your daughter to teach all that follow her to respect the eagle as a creature. You shall also tell her that one day the eagle shall be a symbol for the odd ones she will teach. Only when she has fulfilled this obligation shall her work be done and the debt be satisfied. She shall not die until my entire price is paid. But with any attempt to deviate or abandon the promises you have pledged upon her, she will be destroyed. Be gone now, you have little time to rejoin your pack."

Versa stared at Periphas in astonishment. Annoyed at her silent stare he said, "Was my price too high? No, it was not. It was the bargain we made. You have given your word as a wolf of The First Wolf Pack. Now I have shown the mountain passes such that my part of the bargain has been satisfied, so depart!"

As she turned to the south to begin the long journey back, Versa wondered how this great eagle knew of her daughter. Fear for her beloved Tria and the risk of destruction contained within the strange demand overwhelmed her.

You, too, my friends, may wonder about this mysterious and giant bird. Your civilization has a story of him as well. He is described as a once-great ruler who was turned into an eagle by one greater than himself for being too excellent and too handsome.

Running again for one night and one day, she rejoined the expanded pack while hunting classes neared completion. A little tired and still confused, she found great comfort in seeing the wolf regiment preparing for its last crepuscular hunt, with Tria completely in charge of all her devoted and admiring followers. She joined Arn upon a high place and greeted him with enthusiasm as they looked over their expanded pack and a magnificent plan coming together. She had never held anything back from Arn, nor he from her. But as he asked about her adventure Versa simply said, "Our plan will work. I have found the ways through the great mountains. After the sun sets, each pack leader will be given instructions." She then added, "Tria will receive her direction last."

Knowing her total dedication to their relationship and to their pack, he accepted her partial and mysterious answer without reservation. It is the most fulfilling of relationships when one trusts another even though there is an irresistible mystery put before them. Such was Arn's reaction. He never doubted Versa's ability to always say and do all things exactly right.

32

Very early the next day the alphas called each of their seven fledgling tribe leaders individually. Versa would give Tria the hardest journey, directly through the tallest, deepest, most faraway snow-covered mountains to the north. The mountain valleys and high passes were many times the length and height of the other pathways east and west leading off their homeland peninsula. The other groups had challenging journeys, but Versa knew only Tria could lead her group through the hardest terrain, worst weather, and greatest hunting difficulties. The others would have mountains to traverse but nothing like what awaited her special daughter. Versa took all the various mountain passes learned from the great eagle into consideration as she made the assignments and gave directions to each leader.

To Tria's surprise, Arn and Versa asked her to address the seven wolf pack tribes in a farewell address. Tria spoke extemporaneously: "My brothers and sisters, wolves of the pack, you have within your grasp lives of immeasurable value—value to your pack and value to your race. You will find fulfillment only by your dedication to your pack and to each other. You must trust the alphas, always support each other just as Bord made the ultimate sacrifice, and always live wolf-truth. Each lesson you have learned must never be forgotten. Each of you shall share these lessons with all wolves, everywhere."

With a momentary pause, looking upon her students and comrades, Tria continued: "We all stand upon this momentous day because of two wolves, Arn and Versa. Unselfishly they have shown all of us a more perfect way. While our debt to them may never be adequately repaid, and lo' while it may never be equal to what they have given us, let us all now swear an oath to them that we shall keep The Wolf Ways!"

Cheers of affirmation arose from the entire group without hesitation or limitation. Each newly-formed pack approached the great alpha pair as in a wedding's receiving line; one by one they made their wolf promise never to abandon the ways even unto their death.

With that, each alpha led its untested pack as instructed. No wolf-tear was shed. Versa then excused herself from Arn. He assumed she was off to care for their second litter but watched as she called to Tria. The two then walked off a short way. Now alone and with no risk of eavesdrop, Versa spoke and Tria listened intently. Arn watched as Tria's eyes grew larger and larger in astonishment. He had no clue what was said but had no concern whatsoever that he needed to know unless Versa told him.

Versa shared the great eagle's secret and the promise she made on behalf of her special daughter. Tria sat down, stunned by what she was hearing. Her mother cautiously conveyed that the gift of near immortality came with a steep price: instant death for any betrayal of her bond with Periphas.

Tria replied "My great mother, any promise you make shall be my honor to fulfill. I can do no less than honor you and the great Arn for all you have given me and all other wolves." With that the two exchanged a heartfelt farewell, knowing somehow, they would see each other again.

As Tria returned to her tribe after receiving her mother's blessing, Arn and Versa bid them all farewell and good fortune as all seven tribes departed to find their destinies.

Tria's pack, ever-moving north, found countless, great woolly sheep with sharp horns scaling great rocky cliffsides, and others with rounded horns hard as steel. The easy-to-hunt herbivores of home roamed not at these higher elevations, but with Tria's leadership her pack enjoyed occasional successes, enough to remain well-fed. The penetrating cold did not deter her from guiding her charges over eight snow-covered mountain passes. On the coldest nights, she showed her rabble how to gather in a jumble of warmth just as she had learned in her youth.

As Tria's group reached the summit of the last pass, they grew overwhelmed by the endless vista of smaller rolling hills cut occasionally by various streams and lakes. None, not even their leader, had ever seen a landscape so enchanting. As she and her charges gazed upon the land, Tria looked skyward and saw the soaring of a great bird, higher than she had ever observed before. At that moment, she recalled the promise she made to her mother to always remember and respect the eagle, and her obligation to the other mysterious promises.

The apprentice wolves were overcome by their ability to complete such an arduous journey. The bitter cold of the jagged peaks and high passes seemed unending until that moment when they could finally imagine their better future. Tria's unwavering skillful leadership inspired them to abandon any thoughts of giving up. Even when she had led them through perilous places, they were always adequately fed and remained safe from harm. Each challenge once met, increased their pride in their fledgling pack. They now also gained something even more valuable: a new wolf emotion deeply and indelibly embedded in their wolfenness—loyalty—sprung from respect. Remember my friends, wolf emotions have more to do with respect than yours.

As they moved toward the lush, green, new lands hunting as a pack more efficiently than ever, they discovered that certain beasts in the new territory—similar to the deer they pursued in their original hunting grounds, but larger— proved more difficult to take down. Other beasts with great beards and massive chests roamed in countless herds, and the pack would follow these, only able to overcome the weakest. Giant deer-like creatures with horns like broad, flat rocks could injure and kill if used against a wolf. These animals, tall enough to eat near the treetops, were a most dangerous prey. Only within the pack structure could a wolf hope to kill and enjoy the abundance these giants might bring.

As Tria's pack continued their sojourn to the north, they occasionally adopted a lone wolf along the way. With the pack now at twelve and prospering from the great gifts of Arn and Versa passed on by Tria, there were two original converts who appeared to be ready to mate and lead. Tria had instructed them in all she knew, and they were meticulous in the completion of their learning. It was then that Tria recognized her work with this group was done, so she decided to leave them to their own future of pack interdependence. The Wolf Ways would be inextricably embedded in this group and their progeny would move across the continent. Things had worked exactly as The Magnificent Ones had explained.

The other tribes of The First Wolf Pack would similarly move their ragtag packs in the direction given them by Versa. Packs grew by adoption and only an occasional challenger had to be eliminated until The Wolf Ways were permanently established in the lands to the east and west. Eventually each of the loyal five found a wolf worthy of their union, and so our race eventually covered all suitable, distant, and strange lands. Fic and Casso established domains in the lands south of The First Wolf Pack, and Jett and Ellip to the northeast. Only Tria did not yet have a pack truly of her own as she gave it over to a worthy pair of soon-to-be alpha wolves. Although the males of her pack and the lone wolves of the lush valley were all driven to near madness by her scent, none dared approach her in an amorous way.

One lone wolf tracked her pack for many days, scavenging on any morsel left behind. Tria picked up the scent of this follower and waited for the right time to catch him with her stealth and power. Once captured, she did as The Magnificent Ones had taught her; inhibiting her bite, pinning the interloper to the ground until he submitted. The stranger would become part of the pack, but to Tria's disappointment he too was not suitable for her as her body prepared for reproduction.

Bidding her charges farewell, Tria looked to the south and began to make her way back to her homeland, seeking some unknown destiny. She remained alone except for the tiny creature that often hid within her luxurious fur. Occasionally on Tria's solo return journey, Joy summoned others of The Last, and they lit up the evening darkness and sang to her. Their visits reminded the brave young she-wolf that she was a creature of the pack, again alone but not a lone wolf. With the barren rock well in her past, there was no desolation in her heart anymore. As she traveled, the grandeur of the lands upon which she trod also filled her heart with memories of all that was good.

33

The journey back home always seems shorter than the original excursion. This is true for wolves too. Tria moved quickly, occasionally being invited to visit with packs encountered along the way. To those having grown numerous in members, she taught advanced hunting skills—showing them how to split into two or three groups with precision timing while maintaining mastery of the wind. She also tutored each pack how to improve their long-distance communication. For these more sophisticated lessons she was well-fed in return.

Occasionally, young wolves followed her about their camps, asking whether she was the ghostly one of wolf legend. But Tria only spoke of The Wolf Ways and the joys of pack life. As she traveled, she observed from these camps that truly the age of the wolf pack had arrived.

Sometimes, however, she was called on to settle squabbles between neighboring packs, which she did with her irresistible confidence and irrefutable wisdom. She left all the packs she encountered amazed at her leadership and insight into wolf fairness and justice.

Finally, Tria neared Jett's new domain. Though she called out to her brother, the stunning Ellip's voice beckoned the weary traveler to approach. Tails wagging, she found Ellip's fifth litter of pups had grown into a formidable albeit still youthful gang of seven. They reminded Tria of The First Wolf Pack when days of near-perfect satisfaction reigned. Following the lead of the alphas, the young wolves greeted their famous aunt as well. Thereafter, days were spent with Tria telling her young relations of her five-year-long adventure through the great mountains and beyond. Even Jett was transfixed as they all listened to her incredible storytelling. She told her stories of rugged lands and giant beasts with such realism, the young wolves imagined being there and dreamed of following in her footsteps.

At times, Jett and Ellip excused themselves to go hunting, leaving Aunt Tria to watch over their young wolf posse. Seizing an opportunity at evening story time, one pup asked Tria if she ever met the great she-wolf who wore a crown of blood, a bitch so powerful and ghostlike none could defeat her. They had heard from Jett tales of this magnificent wolf-hero, stories that made them all wish to grow into such a canine monster but never learned her name. All the pups could not help but stare at Tria's right ear and wonder if two wolves could carry the same unusual trait. The bold pup asked a follow-up question: "Aunt Tria, we have never seen a wolf as grand and powerful as you—are you the one who killed fourteen?" Tria, without a lying denial, simply assured the pups: "Such a creature once lived. In fact, I knew her well. But this legendary creature no longer exists; she metamorphosed into another, more excellent creature."

On another such evening, The Last offered a sky-filled exhibition to the pack. With Joy settling happily into her great forepaw, Tria found it perfect timing to teach the young wolves about these creatures. The pups had found the light show most pleasing. All sat transfixed by her description of the sweetly-pleasing aerial actors, bringing much importance to those appearing insignificant by their diminutive size.

As the little light show continued, Tria declared to the young wolves: "These are The Last. When you see them, you will remember the joy of your existence no matter your circumstances, and you will recall the perfection of The Wolf Ways. You will be ever-grateful for the lands upon which you hunt and for the beasts that perish for your benefit. Will you all promise me this?"

The young wolves all clamored in agreement and asked Tria to tell them more. Tria simply explained that these little ones had lifted her spirits while she endured a great struggle. Then with a voice of power that startled all of them she stared into the eyes of each. Tria demanded they accept her words with no hesitation or equivocation. Each young wolf knew she spoke wolf-truth; there would be no more questioning allowed or necessary as they drifted to sleep with blissful hearts.

While the young wolves slept, Tria settled down just on the outer edge of the camp. She decided that tonight she needed answers. With all the creatures in the land knowing of Tria's greatness, it was The Last and Joy that seemed to know first. As Joy flew from out of Tria's paw, she reminded the young leader of her prophecies. Tria took this moment to demand, "Who are you little one and why do you glow like nothing else?"

Joy settled on Tria's prominent black nose and whispered to her, "Now I may tell you, for you are well upon your journey to greatness, although it is far from complete. Know first, we will never abandon you. The things I will tell, you may share with other creatures only when you have kept all of the promises you made to Versa and through her to the mightiest of all birds, the ruler of all blessed with flight."

Tria's mind returned to the great eagle's mysterious demand conveyed by her mother. And she was gobsmacked by this little visitor's revealed knowledge of Periphas and his demands.

Then Joy continued, "Now you shall know of whence we came. When The Creator had rested on the seventh day and looked upon creation smiling with great joy, it was impossible for the earth to not sing out in happiness. So, in the blink of a moment we all were created, bursting from the earth itself, glowing and filling the sky with the light of joy. While weak and insignificant, we carry a special message of great importance. Now every summer evening we tell all fellow inhabitants of The Creator's satisfaction; thus, my princess, we are the last creature created upon Mother Earth. This is why we are called The Last, and this is why I am called Joy—for I represent the joy of creation."

Joy paused and whispered ever so softly, "There will forever be a special bond between The Last and the wolf. Our illuminated show shall remind each wolf of their history, for we fill a unique space between creation and The Creator. It shall place within all who follow you a profound need to seek The Wolf Ways. It is in honor of you, my princess, that this gift of The Last shall be bestowed upon your race."

Tria stood in stunned silence, her heart bursting with happiness and contentment. She had seen much of the continent beyond her own land and beheld all the beauty of great and minor places—of oceansides, streams, mountain ranges, canyons, dense and wet places, dry lands and plateaus, and places of bitter cold and ice. All were beautiful to her. With this she recalled that no matter how many times she felt moved by the beauty of a place, it matched the soaring spirit she felt when The Last appeared to her.

Tria, remembering the humility of Casso and the day of her rescue, then softly spoke to Joy. "May your gift to my race not be in my honor, but in honor of The Magnificent Ones for they are the origin of all good that matters to us. I will always keep your identity in confidence until I have fulfilled all my promises put upon me by my magnificent mother. You, my glorious little friend, have the unbreakable bond of my wolf-word."

Joy had no doubts but rebuked Tria, "It is not for you to decide the dispensation of true honor. As a wolf you need not concern yourself with such things. You shall focus on ever-promoting The Wolf Ways, even in situations you cannot now imagine. Honor shall not be your concern." Tria knew not to argue.

34

A few days later, Tria prepared to set off to honor her sire and dam. As Jett beamed with satisfaction and admiration for his great sister, Ellip and her adolescents begged Tria to return soon. So much had improved in the life of every wolf, everywhere, because of The Magnificent Ones, and especially because of Tria. Jett anticipated the most remarkable reunion for Tria, Arn, and Versa. Coming close to her they renewed their sibling bond in parting—the way only wolves know as sincere and pure. She made her way across Jett's valley and over smaller mountains until reaching the valley of her youth. She scaled the hill where she first met The Last and called out to the founders of all wolf success. And she was welcomed. With more joy than she could remember experiencing she was embraced by them, not as you primates embrace but as we wolves enjoy, with sniffing and wagging of tails. The greeting lasted much longer than one would expect for a wolf, enthusiastically sniffing each other while turning a circle, each chasing the other with no idea who was leading and who was following until suddenly they all sat down simultaneously, bursting out in laughter.

Versa, looking lovingly upon Tria, felt overjoyed with her daughter's size, strength, and wisdom. She reflected on how Tria had transformed from an emotionally immature, maniacal executioner to a great leader who appeared ageless, despite her long journey. Surely no other wolf could ever match Tria's achievements. Admiring their daughter, Arn insisted to Versa that most of the credit was hers, quoting a conversation from long ago: "For the hunt I will lead but for the pups you shall lead." Versa graciously accepted the credit, but both she and Arn knew it was only because of their efforts together this special one overcame her own imperfections.

Versa also knew that while her daughter was the new and ultimate Magnificent One, she would remain incomplete until her genetics and wolf spirit produced new life. They knew Tria must find a male wolf that could live in harmony with her greatness. Arn reassured her: "Surely a perfect mate existed; he need only be found. Because of your legend many will be intimidated by the idea of even approaching you amorously. Do not become discouraged; only those who are powerful, handsome, wise, and confident shall be worth your consideration."

Fortunately, such a male was just then roving toward The First Wolf Pack's domain from the south, hoping to start a pack after his alphas banished him. This lone wolf had been taken in by Fic and Casso when he was only five weeks old, left helpless when his dam lost her life to another lone wolf. As a thunderstorm wailed all through the first night with his new parents, Fic held the tiny male reassuringly within his capable forepaws.

Day after day, Fic's and Casso's adopted pup whom they named Barr, fed on the richest milk. Soon, when about four months old, he would eat from all the bounty of the land. Growing strong on a variety of muscle and organ meats, fruits and other things, he enjoyed all the nutrition a wolf could require. He grew to be solid and powerful. But most importantly, he had learned from them the courage of Casso and the compassion of Fic. And like Fic, the young wolf had the ability to look into the hearts of others as only Fic had done before him. The story of our heroes does not tell us how this one acquired the special sense, whether it was inherent in his nature or learned from Fic the night the thunderstorm bonded father and son in a profound way. Great was his ability to see into the hearts of wolves and men. There are still some among us new-wolves who can see into your hearts. Perhaps you have had the honor to know such a dog.

Barr was taken by Fic when an adolescent to the outskirts of an area where a tribe of your race tended sheep. As they stopped upon a hill giving them a view of all the humans and their flocks, Fic put the question to his young protégé: "Tell me what you see?"

Barr answered, "I see harmless creatures living in harmony."

Fic pressed his youngster, "What of the great bounty awaiting the wolf, almost effortless in the taking?"

Wise in spite of his youth Barr replied: "We have wild lands with all the prey we desire. The creatures we see below are necessary for the survival of the tall ones, as are they for the sheep. The tall ones are weak and slow. The sheep are without defense. Why would I cause either of them deprivation just for an easy hunt?" This legend comes down from Fic and Casso, so we know it is true, but there is more.

Just a year after young Barr's incredible insight into natural harmony, a drought menaced their territory. All creatures grew parched, increasingly agitated, and uneasy. The stress and suffering seemed to go on for several moons. One morning before the sun greeted wolf-senses, Barr arose and promptly addressed his alphas, Fic and Casso. "The earth which lies beneath us is growing restless. The land fights within itself, and the battle grows slowly stronger. I fear it will not stop but increase. I plead with you my great alphas, do not dismiss my concern. My dear father, you, too, might know of what I speak."

With that, Fic ordered his pack to remain in their camp as he sprinted off to the west. Soon after the sun rose, he returned and called Council with The Wolf Utterance. All the young wolves took their usual places in the camp as Fic and Casso walked to a private place.

Only Fic spoke: "It is through the pads of my paws and the hair on the back of my neck that fear now enters my body. My nose tells me of burning smells but not like that of a wildfire. I know our Barr is correct. We shall leave our camp and travel to the mountains under the rising sun; now!"

With that, Council adjourned. The alphas gathered their pack and departed in haste. They traveled two days before Casso picked a place for their new camp.

On a hot night not suitable for sleeping, the earth rumbled, and smoke began to billow from the tall peak that dominated the vacated territory of Fic and Casso. As they looked for Barr to acknowledge his predictions, he was not found among them. Casso, then Fic called out, "Barr, where have you gone?" But they received no reply.

Soon the mountain peak began to convulse with great columns of smoke as the trembling of the earth turned to intense quaking. Fire began to fall from the sky. This fiery hail began igniting dry grasses and scrub woodland as the molten death rained down upon the dry plain from which they had escaped.

Barr sprinting from their new wolf camp before the others woke, had departed just before the tremors began. Running flat out he saw a fast-spreading fire begin to approach the tall ones' huts. He knew their sheep would be nearby. Arriving as hot ash sprayed into the air, exceeding the height of clouds and obscuring the moon, Barr now stood in their midst. Snarling and snapping he forced the sheep away from the flames while the tall ones ran behind screaming and waving weapons. Farther he drove the sheep until he sensed the wind was in his face. He pushed them further into the wind for miles until he reached a sheltered valley. Being weak and slow, the tall ones could not keep up with Barr and the sheep, but they never stopped running. As he finally got all the sheep to safety, he scaled the hilltop to view what he had left behind. Fires scorched the plain and glowing red liquid began rolling down the sides of the shuddering mountain.

The tall ones drew nearer, scaling the last hilltop and descending into the valley to find their flock intact. Soon Barr heard a mother scream hysterically. He stared at the female weak one, peering into her eyes. He understood that one of her pups was left behind. With that Barr raced back to the place from which he had driven the beasts. Running between the nearly converging flames with incredible speed, he pulled the missing tyke out of the now smoldering hut and from imminent danger. Exiting, he split the flames just moments before they unified into a single conflagration. Barr rushed back to the valley of safety and gently placed the baby at his mother's feet. None raised their weapons but stood dumbfounded. Now a spectacularly handsome and mature adult, he would soon be leaving the plain of fire to come north.

The Magnificent Ones and Tria heard calls in the night telling of a most special and great young male wolf on the move and nearby. "Powerful and wise, handsome and reserved, with eyes that penetrated wolf-hearts," the wolf voices reported. "The peaceful and quiet one from the mountain of smoke" was another dispatch carried across the dark sky." A third message also repeated night after night: "A wolf of unequalled endurance, able to travel more than two hundred miles in a day, and capable of tremendous bursts of speed."

All her life, Arn reassured Tria that she would know when a specific male would suit her. As Tria heard these ever-increasing wolf dispatches, with her pheromones raging, she hoped this unusual hero from the south might be the one her sire predicted would be worthy of her greatness. With her physical changes, Tria knew before the asking that it was time to leave Arn's and Versa's camp.

With only one of the surrounding hills taken, the extraordinary she-wolf had six from which to choose. She teased the newcomer from the south with her scent and led him to the hill where she had first met The Last.

Having richly-dark ebony fur, he also had a splash of silver on his chin and chest—a bit of spilled milk and cream filling, if you will. It gave him a friendly and whimsical look to counteract his intimidatingly muscular build, massive head and mesmerizing eyes. As he approached Tria, he immediately realized that the power of both Arn and Versa were upon this she-wolf. And he suspected she might be the ferocious wolf of legend. Certainly, her right ear was singular. Driven by instincts or some special insight, Barr advanced with confidence. He looked into her eyes and Tria felt as if her heart had been laid bare to this stranger. An irresistible pull toward this handsome young male weakened her defenses. Besides the eyes of Fic, his sturdy wolf physique appealed to her body. Though the intensity of her reproductive drive grew overpowering, Tria also felt an upwelling of joy in her spirit, as if a deep and hidden mysterious need within her now demanded this unique wolf become part of her life. There upon the hills of her youth Tria would approve of this one called Barr—she would finally have her own pack.

With many lone wolves relocated to great and minor lands beyond the territory of The Magnificent Ones, enough food for a second pack—that of Tria and Barr—remained. While they would not permanently dwell in Arn and Versa's territory, they were granted permission to stay, at least for a bit.

Arn and Versa could not get enough of Barr. His charm and strength were irresistible. So, the four hunted together and shared their bounty. Soon they all realized Tria had pups on the way and together the four great wolves enjoyed incredible wolf happiness. Many days and nights, as the hunts allowed, they would gather and speak of things that Tria had seen on her journey and discuss her catalog of The Wolf Ways.

One night, Versa asked her daughter, "Tell us Tria, how many ways are there, and did you use them all on your journey?"

Tria replied, "There are twelve ways as I have identified them. All are of great value."

Versa pressed her further, "What is of greater importance, the finding or the teaching? Was it not you who first realized there were certain ways of the pack? Therefore, was it not you who not only found them, but now teach them? It seems to me my daughter, you are The Wolf Ways."

But Tria would not hear of it, saying: "Is the one who simply measures and records the changing tides greater than the sea itself?" Tria had developed such gratitude for her sire and dam that she could not even see that her own greatness had surpassed theirs. For without her, the ways might have never reached beyond the territory of The Magnificent Ones. For without her, only the life of the lone wolf might rule.

Arn and Versa recognized her humility was sincere, but Arn refused it: "Tria, it is not for you to decide on the distribution of honor when you are the hero!" This unexpected chiding by her sire had a familiar ring to it as Tria remembered what Joy had once said to her about the same topic.

Not long thereafter, before another mating season arrived, Tria and Barr relocated their camp just out of reach of the hunting grounds of Arn and Versa, but near enough to check on each other's condition. As summer returned, Tria noticed The Last often hovering upon Arn and Versa's hill. What could it mean?

Upon the hill of Arn and Versa, joy reigned. They had seen their great daughter succeed in her teaching, in her journey, and now with a mate: all their wolf wishes had been met.

Arn spoke to Versa: "You and I have done what no others had done before us. How is it that we fought and did not die? How is it that we have lived in health and prosperity beyond all others?"

Versa pondered these questions and replied: "We are fortunate beyond what we deserve, but some wolves had to be the first to form a pack, otherwise only folly and destruction would be the fate of our race. How it was that you and I were the ones to do so does not matter. What matters most is that The Wolf Ways must be followed forever. And it is by Tria, and now with Barr at her side, that this just might be possible. We now bask in the greatness of Tria." Then the two wolves lay comfortably watching The Last, and they knew complete wolf peace.

One night soon thereafter, The Last covered the entire hill of Arn and Versa, with the light show starting at dusk and not ending until daybreak. This time the sky was filled with an intensity Tria had never seen before. Her heart rang with happiness as she and Barr watched from their camp. Countless members of The Last filled the night as if they wished to levitate the entire hill upon which The Magnificent Ones resided. The following morning Tria and Barr, with their young ones grown enough to remain behind, decided to pay a visit to ask why the lights were becoming so frequent and now so intense.

As they came closer, Tria called out to her parents: "Arn and Versa, it is I Tria. We wish to join you and discuss the things of last night." But she received no reply. Knowing their habits would not have them off their hill at this time, the failure of a reply caused her concern. So Tria looked at Barr and said, "Let's go!" They sprinted the rest of the way only to find Arn and Versa missing.

Barr assessed the situation saying, "No sign of battle. No sign of accident. Just a simple landscape as if no one had been upon that hill for days or more. Even the scent of them is gone." He repeated this again for Tria's sake. Then he said, "While I do not understand why they are gone; I feel nothing but overwhelming peace."

It was then that Tria heard Joy's soft call in her right ear. Ignoring Barr, Joy only spoke to the one she called "my princess."

Joy whispered, "There is much you do not yet know of our creation. There are creatures purer than any others of their kind. Filled with honesty and greatness they are the closest thing to perfection a creature of its species might ever be. Do you understand me, my princess?"

Barr stood motionless as he knew something was happening to Tria. He thought he might be hearing a faint whisper but could not be sure. Then he heard Tria speak in reply. "Little one, I understand your words but not your meaning. Please help me to know what you wish me to comprehend."

Barr could not discern the quiet whispers as Joy continued: "Arn and Versa were such creatures; the closest to wolf perfection in body and spirit. Sometimes these types of souls are needed elsewhere. As with the great bird Periphas, there are few great enough for this second life. Only they can bring that purity to another species in need. Or for very few who are even greater, only they can be the ghostly messengers between the earth and heaven. Such were The Magnificent Ones."

Seeing Tria drop to the ground, Barr ran to her side. She looked at her mate and asked, "Did you hear what I heard?"

Barr replied "No, I did not."

Regaining her composure, she stood and said, "Let's go home. I'll explain it all to you as we go."

While they walked, she relayed Joy's words to him verbatim. Barr tried to comprehend such a mysterious message. Then Tria explained: "While these elders we love are now gone, the only way to honor them is to live out The Wolf

Ways with more joy and dedication than ever." Barr heartily agreed and would never waver from this promise to her.

As Tria reached this, the last milestone of her maturation, she and Barr would enter the truly momentous stage of their legendary lives. Their legacy as history's most prosperous and productive wolf pack would only be the beginning. Our legend tells us they lived together and remained vital for more than one thousand of your years. Their genetics are dominant in all modern wolves and dogs.

35

Year upon year passed, across all suitable lands pups were born, and the most capable of young adults were banished to form packs of their own. Great running wolves built of Tria's and Barr's genetics spread quickly beyond their domain, ever-moving, generation after generation. Pushing further outward, the wolf pack now covered all cold and all temperate lands, even crossing a great land bridge allowing pack life to reach the most distant places. But of all the tribes and their descendants, none traveled down beyond the place where the midday sun cast no shadow.

When it seemed generations of wolves lived a perfect existence such that time should never need to move, messages came across the night skies of battles over territory and of starvation. While these communiques had to travel over great distances, through repetition nothing of importance was lost or distorted. Fortunately, we wolves are known for our accuracy. With all the good fortune brought by the seven tribes carrying The Wolf Ways, still much turmoil brewed in distant, newly-settled lands. As the stories reached her, Tria contemplated how she might help.

It was during one warm and clear evening that The Last spent much time around the camp of Tria and Barr. As Joy appeared, she first introduced herself to Barr, showing proper respect and apologizing for her past rudeness upon the hill of Arn and Versa. Then she flew close to Tria explaining, "We have heard from the great eagle that the battles over territory and starvation of which you hear are true. He has soared above many places to see the conflicts. He sends the message that some have forgotten your ways; others still have not heard your message. You are now grandmother to many; you are the professor of The Wolf Ways, and your ferocious legend remains throughout your species, so it is you who must go."

Lighting upon Barr's forepaw she continued, "You must go with Princess Tria, for your ways and powers make her complete. You, too, must save many." With that Joy and The Last drifted to the hillside just below the camp and sang their illuminated song all night.

From the position of their territory, they could access all lands—but where to go first? Tria recalled how arduous was her first journey directly north through the heart of the mountains, so she spoke to Barr saying, "Let us first go to the far and hard places. After, all else will be easy. I know the valleys and passes and the animals thereupon. We shall be without fear or concern." He, of course, knew she was right—but as they decided to pursue this somewhat unclear mission, neither had any idea just how far they would travel.

Over countless seasons, with their many litters now grown and moved on to their own pack lives, Tria and Barr left their home territory and traveled. It was time again for her to be the professor of The Wolf Ways.

Meeting with packs along the way, they were enthusiastically greeted. These newly-formed packs did not require extensive training, all having been initially taught by wolves of the seven tribes. Nonetheless, every pack wanted Tria and Barr to stay permanently. Touched by the affection but with more travel ahead, visits were kept short, focusing on perfecting each pack's knowledge and practice of The Wolf Ways, long-distance communications, and improving hunting techniques.

Inevitably, everywhere, Tria spoke of The Wolf Ways with the same clarity and passion as she had first done at Jett's rock. All were astounded by her wolf eloquence and vowed to always spread her teachings without hesitation or delay. She often gave her students illustrations of pack loyalty with stories of Bord and Casso. Culminating her speech after the stories of her two heroes, she repeated these words everywhere, "The pack is more than bloodline; it is the loyalty of the wolf's heart that matters most. Cooperation, tolerance, and loyalty are the foundational virtues powerful enough to temper the poisoned blood of hatred that once threatened the very survival of our species. And only with your unconditional embrace of all the things I have taught you, shall you find bravery. Then you shall be wolves of the pack." And every time her audience cheered and came away more dedicated to The Wolf Ways than before.

Occasionally Tria would be asked if she was the legendary ghostly, she-wolf, but Barr always jumped in with a hearty laugh saying, "How could one such as I be alpha mate with a legend?" It became their little joke, and Tria loved Barr all the more for it. When arriving to new wolf territory, Barr would stare into the eyes of the inhabitants and later inform Tria who most needed special attention and instruction.

Reaching some distant places where not even the existence of The Wolf Ways was known, Tria and Barr intervened in squabbles and battles before they could teach The Wolf Ways. Staying much longer in these places, they would raise up their own litter, adding to the vitality of the genetic pool. By design, once grown, their offspring always remained behind as Tria and Barr moved to new destinations. By the time they left each place, even the hostile and difficult, all wolves lived in proper packs.

With all her public speaking, she remembered to keep her promises. Tria never fully explained The Last nor mentioned the name of the great eagle, but these things occasionally nagged at her. Sometimes while traveling, she wondered how long it would take for her to fulfill her destiny. How would she know when to convey the special symbol of the eagle to satisfy her promises? And would she be certain to recognize the odd ones when she met them? Barr, knowing Tria's private thoughts preoccupied her, tried to keep all things in the present as best he could, although he wondered silently to himself about their magical existence, especially their apparent agelessness.

After travels to four of what you call continents over countless seasons, the two heroes finally realized that their work was nearly completed when they recognized they had visited the same territories and family lines on multiple prior trips. Confident they had visited all places suitable for wolf habitation, Tria and Barr were now certain the way of the pack would endure. Having lived longer than any wolves before or since, generations of wolves across the entire earth all knew of the special ones that did not age—the ones who carried the gift of true wolf knowledge and wisdom.

Finally, all their students everywhere had learned how to prosper and live in peace. You must understand that for canines, peace does not exclude conflict, it only detests unnecessary destruction. The Wolf Ways recognizes only the most powerful and pure leaders and tolerates no dishonesty or subterfuge.

Knowing their mission was complete, it was time to return to the territory they once controlled. Perhaps the hill where they first met would be the place to rest. Surely it would be a different place than they had left. Moving now more slowly than when their great sojourn began, each savored every field and wood, each stream and rocky place. While rivers had meandered and trees had grown or fallen, gorges deepened and mountains shifted, the smell of their home remained just as sweet.

Now only days away from journey's end, Joy appeared to them one evening and warned them of the other species that occupied their lands. It, too, was experiencing territorial battles and starvation. Joy stressed to Tria and Barr that the battle of these odd ones, who Tria would come to call the weak ones, could not be ignored. But the wolves only assumed it might mean they would have to scatter your ancestors and send them running.

36

The ancient wolves approached the heart of their homeland. There, a great bitch of many generations descended from Tria—named Ammer, and her mate, Tep—occupied part of Barr and Tria's homeland. While the heroes' hearts ached to see their great-great-granddaughter and her pups, they also recalled Joy's message and wondered what else they would find upon this land.

Tria and Barr were greeted by Ammer atop her hill, the one that was first claimed by Tria. Wolf-hearts burst with joy at their reunion without distraction by the noise of battle below. Effusive licking, tail-wagging and the great sniffing-circle were performed by the four wolves as a suitable introduction of ancient relations. It was their great fortune to meet Tep, Ammer's mate. A grand wolf of calm disposition, Tep reminded Tria of her beloved brother, Jett. Knowing they were too ferocious and strong to be threatened by the two-legged rabble, and safe upon their hill, Ammer and Tep rested and hunted together trying to ignore the weak ones. Day or night, oftentimes they could still hear the clamoring of conflicts between the weak ones in the distance. Ammer, who had only recently whelped a litter of seven, was much troubled by the unnecessary destruction and death suffered by the weak ones at the hands of each other. Still, they allowed the weak ones to reside in a portion of the wolf pack's territory.

These two young wolves now ruled the domain once controlled by Arn and Versa without contender. Even at her advanced age Tria would look at Ammer and see a smaller version of Versa as if she had last seen her great mother just the day before. Ammer even carried a scent similar to that Magnificent One—a complete package of all wolf characteristics, without flaw. As for Tep, Tria could not stop looking at him. Truly he was a wolf's wolf: his body was balanced and strong, his eyes clear and penetrating, his gate like that of the most masterful running wolves. He smelled of power and confidence but also gave off an air of serenity, reminiscent of Jett. Upon their first meeting, he and Barr seemed like they had been close family members for a lifetime.

For all their young life together on the hill, sometimes just before sunrise, these two heirs to the home of the original wolf pack, Ammer and Tep, would have their senses awakened. Something inexplicable permeated their camp. It soaked their souls with feelings of peace and calmness that even squabbles among the weak ones in the valley below couldn't spoil. Ammer focused all her wolf-senses to discover what was upon the camp, but without success. However, there were times when she thought she saw out of the corner of her eye a fleeting glimpse of a pair of enormous wolves. When she turned to look, they were always already gone. Ammer could smell nothing, hear nothing, and see nothing, yet she sensed something. She remained convinced these inexplicable forms hiding in her peripheral vision were real. While such things should have been a source of discomfort, she never felt threatened.

With the arrival of Tria and Barr, Ammer and Tep soon became focused on hunting together again as the wolf grandparents rested and doted on their grandkids. While the magical pair remained vital for the hunt, often they preferred to stay in the wolf camp. After many thousands of miles over hundreds of years traveling the earth and teaching The Wolf Ways, anyone would want to rest, even a maniac high-strung terrier like me.

Tria remembered Joy's words, but she was perplexed. Surely, she could easily chase the weak ones from these lands as wolf packs had done for seasons too numerous to count, but she could not speak to them. How could she fulfill what Joy implied to her? Were these the odd ones of whom Periphas spoke? If they were, how could she lead these creatures of such a different nature? But Tria snapped herself out of day-dream thinking. This was not a time to contemplate ancient prophecies; it was a time to be wolves of the pack.

Ammer and Tep were most eager to be free to hunt large game together again. Being one so completely unselfish and generous, Tria offered to join them while Barr remained guardian of the den. Ammer and Tep were astonished at how quickly Tria picked up a scent or a sound, neither of which they discerned before her. Even at her great age, she moved quickly with a unrelenting purpose at which the two young wolves marveled.

As Ammer and Tep struggled to keep pace with Tria, she led them through a long, damp, thick place that seemed to go on for miles until it opened up to a meadow with a dry stream bed in the distance. Stopping suddenly, Tria glanced at the two young adult wolves and smiled at their surprise. Tria had led them to a place with a quantity of beasts they had not seen before. She bid them well and told them that she would now go back to their wolf camp saying, "This place of great bounty is where I spent very crucial days of my youth. Now that you have found it you, too, shall enjoy its endless bounty." Trotting off, she knew soon they would return to the camp with a feast and more.

Tria had known all that any wolf had ever known, and no other would ever know more. She and Barr had traveled much of her beloved Mother Earth and spread prosperity to her race. With her great legacy of teaching The Wolf Ways across creation, gratitude for her service to her race reigned in her heart. Furthermore, having whelped many litters and with countless progeny, Tria trotted back toward Barr and the little ones filled with boundless joy. Satisfied with life, she realized that now she too lived the *joie de vivre* that made Jett special. All this happiness and satisfaction notwithstanding, Joy's last prophecy and the promise made by Versa on her behalf would not be suppressed from the back of her mind.

Returning to Barr and the camp, she worked among the pups, cleaning them and moving them about for their comfort. As expected, the proud parents returned soon with ample meat, and Tep stated, "At times like this we need a feast." And they did—a great wolf-banquet upon a special hill within a magical land where The First Wolf Pack had emerged eons ago. It was fitting for Tria and Barr to arrive at this special place to close the great circle of the pack and The Wolf Ways.

After their feast, as all slept deeply, Ammer awoke to another glimpse of the two ghostly giant wolves about her camp. This time they strode around her, again and again. Confused but not fearful she looked at the others; they did not stir from their slumber, as if a sleeping potion had been placed upon them. Then Ammer tried to speak to the ethereal beings. Her mouth refused to work. Slowly they stopped their circling and sat before her. They were regal. Majestic.

Beautiful. Peace and joy engulfed her. Then thoughts came to her mind as if they were magically spoken to her without sound. "You are of the famous bloodline of we, The Magnificent Ones. Your wolf-heart is pure; be loyal and generous. You shall help the weak and needy, for this is your destiny." With that the spirits left her.

The next morning, Ammer with enthusiasm and confidence explained to the others: "There are many scents in our land and of the creatures there upon, and I know them all. Now there is one which is vaguely familiar but out of place. It is intensely innocent yet fearful. I shall go see it and know it for it is upon our territory."

Knowing her brood was safe with the other three wolves about, Ammer hoisted her milk-laden body and trotted off into a deep and dark secret corner of the forest. She found a grand and ancient fig tree sitting in a perfect place of sun and water. Many of your kind would learn of this tree and speak of it in a special way. Stepping carefully along the banks of the river that first brought Arn and Versa together, she approached. Next to that fig tree, a great beech tree towered above it protecting the fig from the roiling waters. As she reached the partially-submerged roots of the fig tree, within them she saw two very young and helpless pups huddled together. So incongruous to her experience, Ammer crept toward them cautiously while her keen senses quickly informed her that they posed no threat.

Preoccupied by the visit of the wolf spirits and the thoughts that sprung into her mind the night before, she contemplated the ancient legend of Bord. She knew the story was about more than his courage, the story was also about how The Magnificent Ones accepted a stranger from outside their pack. It also told of finding loyalty without condition. Focused on what lay before her, she pulled the babies from the wet muck and licked them clean. Then she gently lay with them on a dry and soft spot, providing much needed warmth and rich wolf-milk nourishment. After comforting the strange pups, she took them within her immense and powerful jaws, raced to her den, and laid them beside her children.

Within the dark but warm wolf's den, many meals of rich wolf-milk would strengthen the two newcomers. Tria watched, astonished at Ammer's tenderness toward these very young and helpless creatures. It made her joy-filled to be reminded of her brother Fic, the powerful but sensitive one who stood beside her on Jett's great rock—Ammer certainly carried his traits. At that moment, Tria finally realized how she would fulfill one of Joy's prophecies.

Tria spoke to Tep and Ammer, "With your permission, of course, we will stay here upon your hill to help you with these odd ones—they are the babes of the weak ones."

Barr enthusiastically repeated the request: "I know these creatures well. While in their fear they might threaten us wolves, they will also know when the wolf is their brother."

Consent was received from the young alphas, for consent was needed from the alpha pair of the territory even though Tria and Barr would never be denied anything they chose to do by any wolf, anywhere in the world.

Ammer's adopted children ate more, cried more, and proved more helpless in every other way. Their scat was noxious, and they did not know how to avoid their own waste. Eventually, crawling slowly out of the den, they did not pounce and fight like the others, although they watched the young wolves and tried. Perhaps, Ammer pondered, they were just younger than her pups. Tria, however, reminded her of their identity. Years passed and their first littermates moved on to start their own packs, but the two strange ones, growing quite slowly, remained dependent.

While they made many non-wolf sounds, as they grew up they could join the evening's wolf songs that filled the night air with the stories of The Magnificent Ones, a great she-wolf, and a magical pair that spread everywhere the lessons of The Wolf Ways. They demanded milk, which Ammer could not always offer. Slow to wean, they even suckled on dry teats. Soon they learned to devour regurgitated meals from Ammer and Tep.

As the pair eventually became mobile and curious, all four adult wolves protected the young outsiders and guided them in The Wolf Ways as if they were their own. Early one morning Barr departed toward the camps of the weak ones and returned a short time later with pieces of the dried and pounded skins of deer and other beasts, laying them across the bodies of each twin. Soon the little ones learned to cover themselves with gifts of Barr's thievery. Ammer's adopted pair, now standing on two legs, would find as their private tutor the greatest wolf-teacher of all time. Tria took to teaching them in earnest. Always watching and guiding them, Ammer thought Tria might prefer them over her wolf grandkids.

37

Ammer and Tep were living the most unusual wolf pack existence. While it was suspected throughout her homeland that the ancient one, Tria, was the legendary phantom wolf who could not be destroyed, it was not openly discussed, perhaps out of fear or respect. Probably both. And these two wolves, like all other wolves everywhere through the centuries had done, quickly recognized Tria and Barr as the seemingly immortal, legendary teaching pair. Respected and shown hospitality like no other, they were welcome to stay for as long as they chose. It was oddly fitting that also contributing to this most unusual existence of Ammer and Tep was the addition of the two weak ones.

Somehow Ammer knew deep in her wolf-heart that Tria was both that ghostly killer and the progenitor of Wolf Ways perfection that led all wolves to prosper. Gratitude welled within Ammer for her lineage and the opportunity to spend time in the presence of Tria and Barr.

Even after growing a few seasons, the little needy ones could not keep up on the hunts. But of course, running on only two legs, how could they? In a couple more years they learned to trap smaller animals and fish in an attempt to contribute. The four adult wolves sometimes had to control their amusement at the meager fare brought to the pack by the twins. They also brought to the pack slings of cloth containing berries and other fruits not quite a wolf's favorite fare, but edible nonetheless and of surprising nutritional value.

Although they could not contribute to the hunt like her other offspring, Ammer allowed them to stay with their pack across many seasons and new litters, always feeding the strange adoptees and protecting them. After all, it was Ammer who ruled this pack for the pups, but of course she looked to Tria, the mother of wolf wisdom for guidance.

Using her unmatched senses and the skill of stealth, Tria sometimes led the twins to places where they could watch the rabble without detection. These two clever boys learned much by observation. They carefully selected and pounded rocks together creating sharp edges that allowed them to masterfully slice hide from muscle for each kill as one of their contributions to the pack.

One of them always begged to travel to the oceanside where he would watch all the shore birds wander about while the powerful flying predators plied their trade. That same boy would flex his hands, pretending them to be talons to mimic what he saw when prey was taken by the eagles. Barr and Tep would usually take responsibility for this trip, taking the odd twins to see the ocean.

Now completely accepted and valued members of their pack, each year brought growth and strength. Somehow these odd ones found a way to fit in for many years. That was until the day Ammer saw one of the twins, now becoming tall and menacing in his own way, lift a shaft of hardwood from the forest floor and use it in rough play against the skull of one of her young progeny. Ammer growled "You shall not hurt any of our pack that way!" Having a thick wolf skull and the weapon being wielded by a weak one, nothing unfortunate occurred. The weak one dropped the piece of wood and groveled at the feet of the alpha bitch.

It was then that Ammer decided to banish them from the pack. Her growl and stare stopped the dangerous play at the first strike, but it was irrefutable that the time of separation had come. Tria, wishing to support Ammer, gently spoke to her, "You are the ruler of such things. A mother wolf's decision is inherently wise." The wolves knew that the twins, having lived among the practitioners of The Wolf Ways, would find these ways integral to their soon to be independent lives. Also knowing they had gained skills at hunting and toolmaking made all confident in Ammer's verdict.

The twins understood that a change must come, and they did not object but instead were captivated by the chance at adventure. Tria explained "You will find many good things when you join with others of your kind. Do not isolate yourselves but take your chance to be the alphas of your race— you will know when you are ready."

Barr then reviewed with them the certain ways needed to fit in with their new pack: "You must always don clothes and learn the odd language of the weak ones. Until you do, possessing the wolf's ability to read body language, you will understand how to behave in the presence of others without knowing their speech."

Ammer reassured the twins, "Soon both of you will master the odd utterances of the weak ones."

Barr explained further, "Until you learn their language, not by speaking but by being attentive to all they do, they will find you endearing, and you will receive kind treatment. Never fail to peer into the eyes of others. Use your innate sense of reading another's heart as I have taught you." The twins seemed bursting with enthusiasm as their elders piled on instruction after instruction.

With a wolf smile on her face, Tria said, "Do not get close and sniff others as we wolves do. Also remember, among the weak ones your smile does not convey dominance but friendship." After these lessons were dispensed and repeated, Tria escorted the twins to encampments of faraway clans. Then she directed them: "Sneak into the shelters erected by the weak ones. My nose tells me they are not nearby. Carefully explore all that is there; try to understand what you find. Then you are to take better-fitting clothes to make you look less odd to the weak ones." She had taken them far from their camp for the appropriation of clothing so that the weak ones in nearer proximity would not recognize what was worn by the twins. A bit concerned about the stealing, Tria implored them: "Once you have learned how to make or acquire clothes without theft, then you shall give to others who have a need, three times more than you originally took this day." They nodded their obedience to her requirement.

Returning to wolf camp, they used the tools they had fashioned to make each misappropriated piece of clothing fit them well. Their attire complete, Ammer spoke, "Wander along the riverbank nearby, close to our wolf home, so we may be certain of your well-being or rescue you, should threats arise."

Barely teenagers, soon the boys were adopted by a roving band of hunter-gatherers. All the members of the roving band quickly grew fond of these two silent ones so great was their natural wolf-like charm. Handsome and strong, they exuded wolf confidence. But the twins did not like the lifestyle. They resisted the times when they had to roam far from their wolf pack.

Tria diligently kept watch from a distance to verify their odd ones were prospering with their own species. Sometimes she would bring the boys fresh meat to be certain they were well-fed, as every grandmother loves to do. Tria also felt satisfied knowing the twins would share these gifts with their band. And the more ample their food supply, the less they'd need to travel far from her.

Plying their skills and the gifts from Tria, the twins hunted as an isolated pair not allowing any others to join them. With their own tools and using the hunting ways of the wolf pack, they soon provided more substantial bounty than any of the other weak ones, eventually exceeding Tria's donations. With this hunting success, the legend of the silent twins grew throughout their valley and far beyond. The band of weak ones never discovered how these two brought great bounty to the group or how they always knew if a stranger was friend or foe.

38

For the first few years the twins sought out Tria and Ammer to reunite in hidden places known only to the pack. They loved to show their wolf family all they had learned, especially their mastery of human speech. The twins would try to teach their true family how to speak as they had learned to do, but the wolf's anatomy never permitted it. However, while not being able to speak like humans the wolves did quickly learn to understand what was said.

When the twins first left the pack, the great wolves concerned themselves with ensuring the boys' safety among the weak ones. Now, wolf-worry melted away, as they all recognized the twins had established themselves as important members of their adoptive clan. They had mastered speech and even further improved their skills of hunting, leadership, and discernment. With all their successes, nevertheless their secret visits together remained frequent and a source of happiness for all.

With their excellent wolf training, the twins' outstanding powers of observation allowed their quick discernment of other tribes of weak ones whose lifestyle surrounded the harvesting of plants and the keeping of animals. At the same time, they rose to prominence in the affairs of their clan, soon convincing their band of gathers to enjoy supplementing their meat with the fruits of farming and animal husbandry. They had little difficulty in consolidating their clan with another that was already farming, which allowed them to remain within their wolf pack's territory and increase their bounty.

Sometimes the bitches permitted Barr or Tep to join their visits with the twins. On one such visit Tep turned to Tria and asked, "Do you agree that these odd ones might benefit in knowing of the seven great dens of Arn? Perhaps they should learn more of our wolf history."

Enthusiastically, Tria consented, leading them all to visit the original dens of The Magnificent Ones. The twins especially enjoyed the historic tours, entering places no humans understood or dared to inhabit. Even so, these two never felt afraid of these places. Having been fed a wolf's diet and lived a wolf's life hunting mostly in the dark, the twins' eyes did well even when venturing deeply into the recesses of the caves. The boys found interesting the things they observed in the original seven dens. They noticed that while most were pleasantly cool in the summer and warm in the winter, two dens were dug more deeply but then unexpectedly redirected upward. Here, warm water had found its level at the lowest points, allowing the twins to enjoy a most pleasant, warm bath.

After returning to their wolf camp, Ammer called forth a strong young wolf pup from her last litter. His name was Ast. He bonded with the twins immediately and they to him. One of the twins asked, "Why is this little wolf the only one you called to us, mother?"

Ammer replied, "We wish you to have one of your wolf relatives with you. He will be at your side to remind you of The Wolf Ways and protect you. He is the dominant one of this litter, having all the gifts of our ancestors." The twins were thrilled.

The other twin spoke joyfully: "We miss the feeling of wolf fur against our cheeks and lips. We long to feel again upon the skin of our hands the texture and warmth, as we stroke the powerful wolf physique. We want to smell the scent of a wolf brother and for that brother to examine our scent with his discerning nose."

Ammer again spoke: "Shall not our races be joined together for the betterment of all? Shall we prosper together rather than alone just as The Magnificent Ones taught our race? Yes, it can be so—then let us start out as we mean to go."

As they contemplated her words, she spoke again: "By establishing The Wolf Ways within the human race our two species might together live a shared existence of true cooperation, tolerance, and loyalty. All our lives might then be filed with the success of persistence tempered with discernment, and all based in honesty." Ammer went on, "Surely the cunning and strength of the wolf combined with the creativity and intelligence of the weak ones, when joined by and through The Wolf Ways, we will live together in abundance and peace." Tria blinked and nodded approval, most pleased with her great granddaughter's wisdom and generosity. Barr, not so much.

Quite unexpectedly, the next evening Barr called The Wolf Council, startling all. No one dared challenge this great, ancient, reserved wolf's right to call a Council, for so boundless was his wisdom and strength. Yet all were surprised by a call to Council when made by a wolf of few words.

The adolescent wolves of Tep's and Ammer's last litter nervously waited with anticipation as Barr led the four great wolves to his chosen place of tranquility for The Council. There he told them of what he had seen many ages ago when he and Tria traveled to all suitable lands, teaching all wolves. He had seen places where young wolves were captured by the weak ones and put to work as beasts of burden, or worse yet, raised in captivity for food. All listened, astonished, but did not doubt him—except for Tria.

"When did you see such things Barr?" she demanded. "I never saw such abuse while we traveled the continents together."

Barr carefully explained: "While you were teaching legions of wolves after my insight into their hearts was shared with you, I used my gifts of speed and endurance to explore vast areas. I saw much that hurt my soul. Sometimes I would force the weak ones to free our wolf relatives from their captivity." Barr went on to say that he had freed countless wolves from captivity over centuries.

This information suddenly triggered Tria's memory. She recalled a time when she found Barr with a strange wound upon his right haunch. As she licked the wound, she questioned Barr about its cause, but he would only say, "I saw a lot of bad shit." Tria did not bring up the odd event of Barr's wound, but remembering it allowed her mind to rest.

And then to her shock, as if Barr had just read her mind, he looked at his beloved Tria, startling her by saying, "It came from a spear thrown by a weak one. Of all the countless brothers and sisters I freed from bondage, only once did the weak ones inflict harm upon me."

Barr continued with the reason he had called the meeting: "One of the twins has something in his heart that differs from the other. It is an odd reaction to others of his kind. Perhaps Ammer's gift will help him have only the heart of the wolf pack. We must also stay near the twins so they will not lose their way." All sat quietly, contemplating Barr's revelations.

Tria realized that her beloved Barr's decision to not address her question about his wound when first asked (perhaps a couple of centuries ago) was much like her early questioning of Joy of The Last—it was not time for the one asking to know the answers. Knowing wolves do not lie, and that Barr was among the wisest of all wolves, she readily bowed to his conviction.

Her heart filled with respect and admiration for his wisdom when she realized what would have happened had she had the burden of knowing the answer at that time. Surely if Barr had informed her of the wolf abuse by the weak ones when it occurred, this generous professor of The Wolf Ways might have reverted into the ghostly she-wolf no one could destroy. And with Tria's ability to inspire and lead, legions of wolves might have been dispatched to destroy all the weak ones everywhere. No weak ones could have escaped detection by wolf noses, ears, and eyes. Nor would they have survived anywhere on earth should Tria have put her mind to inciting their destruction.

Tria was snapped out of her recollections and back to the Council when Barr proclaimed, "If we are to follow Ammer's plan, we must also follow the example of The Magnificent Ones. Perhaps sharing only one of our species with the twins will not suffice to ensure our races will prosper together. The great Arn and Versa sent seven leaders to establish seven wolf tribes across all lands knowing that it would take many to ensure success. So, it must be with the wolf's adoption of the weak ones." Barr had reasoned that if one of the twins had impurities of spirit, a pack would be more of an influence than a single wolf.

Then Tria responded: "Barr speaks wolf truth; each of the six other original tribes must send a young wolf to join Ast. When the twins enjoy the power of The Wolf Ways with seven great wolves at their side, surely harmony will reign in both worlds. Generations of wolves and men will grow and together become one in The Wolf Ways." With that, The Council adjourned, and their plan could begin.

Messages of the strategy rang out across night skies to all wolves everywhere, carrying the imprimatur of Tria and Barr, and soon young wolves from the other tribes were enthusiastically brought to the land of seven hills.

39

For many months the twins and their pack of the seven tribes met with Tria and Barr to study The Wolf Ways. The great and ancient wolves first taught the young wolves cooperation, tolerance and discernment, how to hunt, and the inhibited bite, along with the alpha role. But in the case of this new partnership, they explained the alpha could be either wolf or human. Either way, perfect loyalty and truthfulness would always be required.

From this point our lives together truly began. It was the gift of Ammer and the seven pups of the seven wolf tribes that is the key to the story your history fails to tell. The wolf had taught your species The Wolf Ways, and most importantly, the seven wolves joined the twins of their own free will.

For several years after the twins had found success, Ammer and Tria would still call to them in a language only the wolves and the twins could understand. Occasionally, Barr would tell other packs through nighttime serenades of these two strange ones and their mounting achievements. Wolf word spread across great distances with the curious story of the twins' and the seven wolf pups' beneficial union. Because of this, soon wolves across the earth contemplated allowing individuals from their packs to join with your forefathers.

With loyal and powerful wolves at their side, the now adult twins brought many gangs of weak ones together into a larger and more prosperous community. None of the weak ones had ever known leaders so youthful, yet so wise and strong. These young men and the seven wolves were of one spirit and mind enabling them to control and guide many. They knew how to dominate others, most often without killing, and for this they became both respected and admired. At times blood was shed when foolish clan leaders refused to submit to the twins, the new and mighty alphas of the weak ones. With uncooperative rulers out of their way, soon consolidation of the area was complete with members of other groups eagerly joining the rapidly growing and prosperous community.

Not long after their domination of all local tribes, the twins also reasoned to drain swampy land to expand their access to the sea, which allowed them to trade with seafarers from across the great ocean. The twins directed the development of the improvements needed for a functional port and learned much from the visitors of different and unusual places with whom they now traded. Wolf-shrewd and able to read the hearts of their new trading partners, ever-expanding abundance continued to be enjoyed by all.

The twins had brought about a rough peace and new prosperity to the hills and the valley near the river and beyond. The weak ones soon flourished in great numbers, thankfully needing far less land for themselves than wolves. Their accomplishments quickly multiplied until they, like Arn and Versa of centuries before, had dominion over the lands they chose.

The river of this story, running down from the mountains and providing drink for all earth dwellers below, is now called by your race, Fiume Tevere—The River Tiber. It was the place where Arn and Versa first fought, then cooperated to raise up The First Wolf Pack. Your ancestors lived upon its banks in small family groups. Inferior to the wolf in strength, vision, hearing, and sense of smell, they slowly grew in number by developing and using the intellectual capacity of their large brains and the viciousness of their hearts. Humans slowly began to problem-solve by watching the predators around them, but lacking the speed and power of the wolf, they instead developed tools. When the twins, known to your history as Remus and Romulus, appeared on the scene of your fledgling civilization they also had the advantage of The Wolf Ways. With seven powerful wolves of the same mind at their side, along with the special gift of The Wolf Ways, they gave rise to a great civilization within the city of seven hills you call Rome—eventually becoming the Roman Empire.

The twins remained loyal to Tria and Barr, as these two ancient wolves stayed near, always permitted within their burgeoning city. Remus declared Tria and Barr to be royalty and required all citizens to treat them as such. The two wolves walked freely on their visits to the twins while the residents always gave them wide berth. But for visits with their wolf-mother, the young leaders would travel to a place known only to them and their beloved Ammer. Time together would refresh each in mind, body, and spirit.

All Romans except the twins, feared the wolf's power and did not understand why these two had complete license to roam as they wished. But they also feared to question their leaders, for so great was the dominance of the twins. The second year after the ancient ones joined the twins in their residence and city—even though the citizenry did not yet know of their special childhood relationship—Remus commanded his agent read a declaration establishing a festival for all to celebrate in honor of these two special wolves. The festival Lupercalia was established, but the people would never understand its true origin or the need to honor the wolf and the wolf-heroes Tria and Barr. Our ancient wolves however, eschewed the idea of a festival. Wolves do not know self-congratulation or self-promotion.

These heretofore ageless ones, now back in the place of their beginnings, no longer teaching The Wolf Ways across the world, now given fame and honor, lost their purpose. Vitality of body and brightness of eye began to slowly dwindle. Tria and Barr spent some days with Remus and Romulus in their grand residences and other times they all journeyed together to visit the special places of the twins' youth.

On one such trip the four of them were joined by Ammer and Tep. Tria took them to that place where the forest met the roiling river and the beech sheltered the fig tree—the place Ammer had first found the twins. Tria looked up and saw a majestic eagle aloft, its sharp eyes searching for movement. This sparked her recall of the promise her mother Versa had made to the great eagle centuries ago. Inspired, Tria spoke to the twins: "You must promise me this, my children; you will use the image of the eagle, that magnificent bird, as the emblem of your fledgling nation-state."

Not understanding the existence of the ancient underlying promise made by Versa to Periphas, Remus objected. But Tria refused his suggestion that the wolf be their image instead. "No, my dearest child, it is my wish the great bird be your symbol to your entire race." Romulus, however, was quick to affirm her wishes and reluctantly Remus concurred.

While all reveled, lingering in the place of their outing, Tria called to Ammer to join her in a stroll along the river to the ancient fig tree. As they approached the place of the historic rescue, and just as Versa had spoken in confidence to Tria centuries ago, now Tria spoke to Ammer. "Promises have been made and they must be kept. All wolves must keep their word. Do you believe this, my granddaughter?" Ammer, a bit confused as to why Tria would ask about the obvious, simply nodded in the affirmative. "The Magnificent Versa placed two promises upon me, which I have done my best to keep. Now that I have satisfied the first promise, which is no concern of yours, I must share with you the secrets of Joy and The Last so that I may satisfy the second of my obligations."

More than a thousand years prior, Versa gave a similar speech to a young Tria before sending the young wolf into the impenetrable Alps. Ammer sat transfixed, stunned, as the full story of Tria's life was unveiled. Detail by detail, event by event, Ammer learned the entire history of The First Wolf Pack, the rock of desolation, and The Last. When Tria completed her account, Ammer sat in silent respect, over-whelmed by a flush of admiration, humility, and hope.

Finally, Ammer spoke: "My life shall be dedicated not only to The Wolf Ways, but also to the history of The First Wolf Pack. I may not deserve to be in your service, but you have honored me as your wolf historian. Therefore, I shall never let you down. I pledge my life to teaching all who follow me. They will all know this great wolf legend." Then slowly, together, side by side, these two alpha bitches rejoined the group. It was time for Ammer and Tep to return to their wolf camp.

When the twins returned to the city together with Tria and Barr, Romulus called in their senior craftsman and ordered "You shall fasten a staff of the finest hardwood and place upon it a golden *Aquila*, the likeness of an eagle clad in gold. We will carry it in front of our legion as the symbol of our power and greatness. The *Aquila* shall be unveiled and used to commence the upcoming new festival."

As he said this Romulus gripped his hands together, mimicking talons. The ancient Barr felt his heart sink as he now more clearly recognized this odd one's propensity for unnecessary aggression. He recalled Romulus's fascination with the eagles as they hunted from the sky unsuspecting quarry below, how Romulus found it especially thrilling watching the bird's powerful talons grip as it dismembered and devoured its prey. Barr realized this was the subtle thing that he had seen in the eyes of Romulus. It was an incomplete development of the values of tolerance and discernment, now recognized by Barr as a possible barrier to full dedication to The Wolf Ways. He felt quite certain that even the seven wolf pups—the gifts of the seven wolf tribes—would not been enough.

Shortly after the declaration of the new holiday, to be held the following month upon its full moon, the twins watched the two legendary wolves suddenly and quickly age.

40

Almost daily now, two gray muzzles rested on the laps of the twins with gentle strokes and sweet whispers from the two who had risen to rulership. Even Romulus seemed to possess gentleness as he held Tria's head and muzzle within his powerful hands. The twins stroked the wolves and nuzzled their faces with their lips and cheeks as they had done when living in the pack. With each passing day and as their bodies weakened, the wolves sought more time with their adopted sons.

Now concerned with the condition of Tria and Barr, Ammer and Tep were seen by many around the seven hills, close to the structures built by the weak ones. At night they called out to the ancient ones with songs of gratitude, concern, and devotion. Barr always replied, "It is we who are the most fortunate ones."

As the twins found their wolf grandparents again within the Royal Forum fast asleep at sunrise, Remus spoke to

Romulus. "Where then are the greatest of wolves? Where are those powerful creatures that protected us, taught us? Where are the ageless and wisest of all creatures?"

Romulus looked at his brother saying "Each day I feel the strength leave them. My heart can bear it no more." And he wept. It was the only time Romulus ever wept.

Over the next week, wolves from the fields of fire, from the Po Valley and beyond arrived in haste, surrounding the seven hills. Soon hundreds of wolves inhabited the river valley. Their presence, especially their mournful songs at night terrified all the residents, except for Remus and Romulus who became emotional with each night's songs.

The next day with broken hearts, as the twins looked into the eyes of Tria and Barr, the great leaders knew the time had come for our hero and her partner to take their rest and join the Great Wolf Spirit.

On a pleasant summer morning when the rising sun made flying hearts fill with wonder, and while in the arms of the twins, each of the ancient ones together gave up their spirits. Remus thought he saw something like columns of illuminated smoke emanate from each, pausing briefly above their lifeless bodies before disappearing. Romulus did not.

The visiting wolf multitude howled endlessly as they thrashed about, not knowing how to control their grief, sensing the passing of the greatest of all wolves. Then amid the hubbub, Ammer stepped upon a high place and called to them: "Wolves of the pack, hear me. Let us honor the ancient ones, the saviors of our race by living out The Wolf Ways as they taught them to us. By our wolfenness, let us swear an oath to never allow them to be diminished or forgotten." Silence fell upon the congregation of wolves. She continued: "Grief never was and shall never be part of The Wolf Ways, only gratitude and loyalty shall fill your heart. Let your life be your honorarium to Tria and Barr. Will you join me in this wolf-promise?"

The crowd of wolves erupted in agreement, howling in unison "Now we shall return to our territories to live and teach The Wolf Ways forever. There shall be no other way for the wolf." With that, they proudly trotted to their own territories to faithfully keep their promise.

The twins, hearing all that was said by the wolves, did not reply to Ammer's calling; their grief remained insatiable. Instead, tears welling up in his eyes, Remus called to the servants: "Bring the finest *klinai* immediately." It was the most impressive royal couch, adorned with bronze, copper, gold, and silver. Then over his gentle sobbing Remus directed again, "Wrap our wolves in the finest silk. Use the royal cloths, the ones edged with gold and beaded with precious gems. Each of my wolves shall have the best regal garment. But first cover them in the royal balm of burial—myrrh and aloe, as is our custom."

The servants hastened to do all that was commanded. After completing the preparation, he instructed the servants, "Carefully place their covered bodies on the couch, gently lay them together so they might cuddle each other in death as they would have slept together in life."

That evening, led by the twins, and with Romulus carrying the golden *aquila*, the servants used the *klinai* to carry Tria and Barr through the entire city for all to honor. With bronze torches ablaze set into brackets on each of the four corners of the *klinai*, the funeral procession finally took them to the outskirts of the city. Remus called out to the funeral procession he and Romulus had led: "Now you shall all remember this evening. Each year you shall celebrate the wolf on this night of the full moon in this, the month of the wolf. Now depart from me and Romulus. Where we go you may not go." Dismissing all the servants and handing the aquila to a servant, the twins waited until they were alone. The seven wolves of the seven tribes howled a lonesome song as they grew restless in their kennels, wanting, hoping to join the last stage of the funeral procession. But selfish in their grief, Romulus and Remus denied their loyal pack the one desire—to pay respect to Tria and Barr.

The twins extinguished the torches, ensuring no one would see their path of travel or destination. Hoisting the ornate platform on their own stout shoulders, a small pleasant green light flickered above the bodies of the two wolves. The twins were soon joined by Ammer and Tep, who walked at their side. Being together in this most solemn task gave all four much comfort.

Together they found a most sacred and secret place to lay the once-great bodies of their adoptive grandparents. Having visited all the ancient dens dug by Arn and Versa, the four found the one place, deepest and most hidden of all, for the final rest of their beloved. So subterranean was the depth of the cave even the near-wolf eyesight of the twins was not sufficient for them to advance. But Joy, having watched over these two great wolf-heroes for centuries, followed the twins into the great cavern and called to others of The Last to join them to illuminate the way to the secret place. Soon the interior shone as brightly as midday.

Romulus and Remus stayed there tearfully howling their goodbyes in the language of the wolf. Dropping to their hands and knees they nuzzled with each other, Ammer, and Tep, just as they had done countless times while living in the pack. Ammer addressed them all: "No beings in all of creation have been as great as these two. They have saved the wolf from loneliness and bitterness. They have taught The Wolf Ways to all wolves and to you also, my beloved odd ones. Do not feel sorrow and grief. These are not part of The Wolf Ways. You must honor Tria and Barr with a life of gratitude for having known them. You must teach The

Ways to your kind so that together all may live in peace and prosperity."

With that, Joy descended onto a patch of warm wolf fur just near Ammer's right ear. She spoke so softly that the others could not hear the details. "You are wise like the first Magnificent Ones. You have fulfilled the request the ghost-wolves made on your hill. And your heart is wise and pure like that of your great-grandmother; be at peace, Ammer." Joy continued, "Just as it was with Arn and Versa, the spirits of Tria and Barr are too great to cease in their service to creation. Perhaps you shall see them again."

Reassured in her own heart, Ammer partially shared with the others what she had just been told, "Spirits such as these are too great to cease in their service to creation." This seemed to speak to all in a comforting way. They took their spots near the *klinai* and sat in silence until the full moon began its descent toward the western horizon. Then they left the secret cavern with The Last lighting their way out of the earthly tomb. Ammer and Tep, shunning grief, returned to their camp maintaining a wolf-trot befitting their wolf pride in having been born of the line of Tria and Barr.

Emotionally devastated and now without wisdom's source the twins traveled back to their city, leaving their beloved wolf grandparents in that secret place covered in wealth and lying on the finest furniture. One small member of The Last stayed behind, burrowing her way under the fine garments to join with those she loved the most. For Joy was true to her word to never abandon Tria.

After the long trek back, approaching the city gates, the twins felt a great rumbling under their feet. A belch of smoke erupted; the distant southern sky glowed a sinister red as lightning flashed and crackled within the volcanic cloud. It would not be the last time their precious Mother Earth would convulse near the place of Barr's youth, the plain of fire.

Pausing at the entrance of the city, ignoring the tremors, Remus turned away from the distant destruction of billowing ash to look back at the special place they had selected for Tria and Barr. He saw a serene night sky filled with countless lights of the softest green, blinking, rising, and descending but never stopping. In astonishment Remus thought these lights kept increasing, even until they outnumbered the stars in the sky.

Soon Romulus and all the residents of Rome flooded into the streets, finding a red sky of destruction to the south and feeling the growling of the earth. Quickly, however, everyone's attention was drawn away from the violence instead to the northern sky, even ignoring the seven wolves of the seven tribes as they broke from their kennels and wandered loose in the streets. But all, the wolves and the weak ones alike, irresistibly stared at the peaceful sky, captivated by The Last's farewell symphony.

Our legend explains how The Last honored these greatest of Canines with the most magnificent display ever produced, even surpassing that which Tria observed over the hilltop camp of The Magnificent Ones, the night Arn and Versa were called to service of The Creator.

It continued throughout the night until the quantity of the miniature lights covered more than the entire hill, now obscuring the sky above the renowned wolves' grave. The growing arc of blinking green lights soon spanned from the eastern to the western horizon, and upward towards the North Star—the earth and sky had joined in a loving burst of gratitude, bidding farewell to creation's two greatest heroes. In respect that night, even the distant volcano ceased its explosive fury.

In honor of The First Wolf Pack, let us all—wolf, dog, and man—remember the words of Ammer: "Wolves of the pack, hear me. Let us honor the ancient ones, the saviors of our race by living out The Wolf Ways as they taught them. By our wolfenness, let us swear an oath to never allow them to be diminished or forgotten."

Epilogue

The Great Wolf Spirit has given me one final instruction—explain to you certain parts of wolf history to provide you further insight into what you have come to believe.

The region of Barr's childhood home, over one hundred miles south of Rome that wolves called the plain of fire, is a massive caldera under the Bay of Naples. Known as Campi Flegrei or The Fiery Fields, it is estimated to have two dozen craters and volcanic structures, some underwater. The area's most notorious volcano, Mount Vesuvius, is famous for the AD 79 eruption that destroyed the Roman cities of Pompeii, Herculaneum, and Baiae.[1] It was during a minor eruption that Barr, many centuries before, saved some of your kind along with their sheep. The landscape there may shift upward or collapse downward based upon the subduction of the African Plate under the Eurasian Plate. We wolves, and other animals, know when the ground beneath us is changing.

There are countless stories of wild animals disappearing from an area just prior to cataclysm like a tsunami or earthquake. This is how Barr knew when to act to save his pack, and then the weak ones.

Romans dug tunnels to capture the heat of the magma conducting through layers of the earth. They also accessed and redirected sulfurous geothermal springs by their tunneling and engineering techniques, eventually creating hot spring baths. The famous Roman baths of antiquity were warmed by geothermal forces first discovered by Remus and Romulus in the dens of Arn. The avid interest in grand engineering feats like tapping the hot springs, and building viaducts was inspired in the founders of Roman civilization when Tria led the twins to view the seven dens of Arn and Versa. Some eight or nine hundred years after Ammer's rescue of the twins, oppressed inhabitants of the city of seven hills would find refuge in the great dens first dug by Arn, expanding them to create the catacombs.

That one brother (Romulus) turned on the other (Remus), committing homicide—your folklore is correct. But you have two versions of your legend. First, Romulus killed Remus when they disagreed on what name to give their city. Romulus, of course, chose Rome, for he wished to name it for himself. But we wolves know that Remus wanted to name it Amore, for the love of their wolf-mother, Ammer. The alternative version of your legend says the brothers disagreed upon which hill to locate the center of their new city—Remus preferred Aventine Hill, while Romulus preferred the Palatine Hill. Romulus, unwilling to have any way but his own, began to build a city wall on Palatine Hill. When Remus climbed over the new wall, Romulus killed him. However, wolf history tells us that both your versions are correct, for Remus climbed the wall to discuss with his brother both the city's name and seek expansion of the wall to incorporate Aventine Hill. With the innocent blood of his brother on his hands, Romulus profoundly and permanently lost his way. Soon he began to plunder nearby cities and capture some of their residents. Eventually, Rome suffered reprisal attacks led by the armies of these other cities. The once defeated Sabines of the city called Cares, successfully attacked Rome, pulverizing its walls and gates. Thus, Romulus was forced to share his king's throne with the Sabine leader, Titus Tatius.[2] Losing his alpha status was proof that Romulus ceased adhering to The Wolf Ways.

Within the City of Rome, executions of traitors and other high criminals were carried out on a place called The Tarpeian Rock located on the south elevation of Capitoline Hill; we wolves know it was first called the rock of desolation. For wolves it was a place of great despair produced by ignorance and self-pity; for us it was not a place for killing.

The eagle (*aquila*) was chosen as the first symbol for the Roman Legions. Roman historian, Pliny the Elder identified five major legion symbols: the eagle, the wolf, an ox with a man's head, the horse, and the wild boar, with the eagle being the first. Roman Consul Gaius Marius undertook an extensive military reform in 104 BC in which the four other standard symbols were eliminated. Only the original, the eagle remained.[3] This is how we know Versa told Tria about the promise made to Periphas, and that she fulfilled it.

Greek legend speaks of a giant, golden eagle that was once a mortal king named Periphas. His wise and virtuous rule was so celebrated that he became admired by many, even like a god. This made the god Zeus jealous and angry. Just as Zeus was about to destroy Periphas, the god Apollo intervened by transforming the king into an eagle. Apollo then set this eagle next to the throne of Zeus. Soon he was adopted by Zeus as his personal messenger and animal companion. Now you know how the northern-bound tribes of The First Wolf Pack could easily get through the Alps.

The world famous bronze statue of the she-wolf suckling two human babies can be found today in The Capitoline Museums in Piazza del Campidoglio, on Capitoline Hill in Rome. While you may call her Lupa, we wolves know her true name is Ammer. The bronze casting does not closely resemble its beautiful inspiration, but at the very least, it commemorates the rescue of Romulus and Remus. The first-born son of Romulus, seeing his father's grief and moved by the story of Ammer, swore an oath to cast her likeness in bronze for permanent display in the seat of power. Though his promise went unkept by him, the folklore lived on—a partial and somewhat inaccurate portion of the legend of Ammer's rescue of the twins would survive. Eventually, many generations removed, an heir to Romulus finally fulfilled the casting promise. The famous historian Titus Livius, in *The History of Rome* said the original statue was exhibited in a place of honor between Palatine and Capitoline Hills around 295 BC.

This, my friends, is the history of The First Wolf Pack.

(1) Wikipedia: https://en.wikipedia.org/wiki/Phlegraean_Fields
(2) Wikipedia: https://en.wikipedia.org/wiki/Titus_Tatius
(3) Wikipedia: https://en.wikipedia.org/wiki/Aquila_(Roman)

Acknowledgements

Special thanks to the following individuals who supported me and helped make this, my first novel, possible:

Publisher Barbara Reed of Terra3 Communications, who guided the completion of this work in countless ways with boundless skill, patience, and determination;

Copy editor Michele Aschkenase, PhD, who guided me in how to communicate more artfully and clearly;

Cover and graphic artist, Rafael Andres, who created the unique cover design and illustrated map, giving the visual impact needed to bring this work to life;

Four beta readers: Andrew Hochberg, Alex Silvergrove, Tony Rubino, and Donna Tropp, who generously reviewed my draft manuscript helping to identify gaps in the story and my blind spots; and to Bill Keeley who generously provided me with draft manuscript production resources and assistance.